RAVES FOR
*Love! Valour!
Compassion!*

"This kind of solid, serious comedy that Broadway hasn't seen in years. . . . It's a hit." —VINCENT CANBY, *New York Times*

"If you're looking to celebrate the vibrant life of off-broadway, start right here." —RICHARD CORLISS, *Time*

"One of McNally's very best plays . . . thick with event and long, it seems to slip by in a few bright-colored minutes." —MICHAEL FEINGOLD, *Village Voice*

"An amazing new play, heartfelt and stirring." —MICHAEL KUCHWARA, Associated Press

"The humor is uproarious and the pathos abundant and genuine." —HOWARD KISSEL, *New York Daily News*

"One of the major plays of our time." —LINDA WINER, *Newsday*

AND FOR
A Perfect Ganesh

"As close to perfect as McNally has come in his distinguished body of work." —*The Times* (London)

TERRENCE McNALLY is the author of numerous plays and TV scripts including the Tony Award–winning book for the musical *Kiss of the Spider Woman*, the Broadway hit *The Ritz*, and *Frankie and Johnnie in the Claire de Lune*, which was made into a feature film starring Al Pacino and Michelle Pfeiffer. His other notable works include *Lips Together, Teeth Apart* and *The Lisbon Traviata*. McNally has received two Guggenheim Fellowships, a Rockefeller Grant, and a citation from the American Academy of Arts and Letters. He also serves as vice president for the Dramatists Guild, the national organization of playwrights, composers, and lyricists.

Love! Valour! Compassion!

and

A Perfect Ganesh

TERRENCE McNALLY

Love! Valour! Compassion!

and

A Perfect Ganesh

Two Plays

A PLUME BOOK

PLUME

Published by the Penguin Group
Penguin Books USA Inc., 375 Hudson Street, New York, New York 10014, U.S.A.
Penguin Books Ltd, 27 Wrights Lane, London W8 5TZ, England
Penguin Books Australia Ltd, Ringwood, Victoria, Australia
Penguin Books Canada Ltd, 10 Alcorn Avenue, Toronto, Ontario, Canada M4V 3B2
Penguin Books (N.Z.) Ltd, 182–190 Wairau Road, Auckland 10, New Zealand

Penguin Books Ltd, Registered Offices:
Harmondsworth, Middlesex, England

First published by Plume, an imprint of Dutton Signet,
a division of Penguin Books USA Inc.

First Printing, September, 1995
10 9 8 7 6 5 4 3 2 1

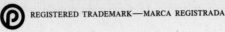 REGISTERED TRADEMARK—MARCA REGISTRADA

LIBRARY OF CONGRESS CATALOGING-IN-PUBLICATION DATA

McNally, Terrence.
[Love! Valour! Compassion!]
Love! Valour! Compassion! and a perfect ganesh : two plays /
Terrence McNally.
p. cm.
ISBN 0-452-27309-9
1. Gay men—United States—Drama. 2. Women—Travel—India—Drama.
I. McNally, Terrence. Perfect ganesh. II. Title. III. Title: Perfect ganesh.
PS3563.A323L6 1995

812'.54—dc20
95-9855
CIP

Printed in the United States of America
Set in Times and Gill Sans Light

Designed by Steven N. Stathakis

PUBLISHER'S NOTE: This is a work of fiction. Names, characters, places, and incidents either are the product of the author's imagination or are used fictitiously, and any resemblance to actual persons, living or dead, events, or locales is entirely coincidental.

BOOKS ARE AVAILABLE AT QUANTITY DISCOUNTS WHEN USED TO PROMOTE PRODUCTS OR SERVICES. FOR INFORMATION PLEASE WRITE TO PREMIUM MARKETING DIVISION, PENGUIN BOOKS USA INC., 375 HUDSON STREET, NEW YORK, NEW YORK 10014.

Love! Valour! Compassion!
was originally produced by
The Manhattan Theatre Club
on November 1, 1994

A Perfect Ganesh
was originally produced by
The Manhattan Theatre Club
on June 27, 1993

SOME THOUGHTS

Plays are meant to be seen, not read, and yet we playwrights are always moaning how difficult it is to get our plays published. In fact, we moan about that almost as much as we moan how difficult it is to get our plays produced. Of course, the thing we moan about most is how difficult it is to write them.

That's a lot of moaning.

The truth is probably that none of it has ever been easy—writing, production or publication—but in these last fleeting moments of the twentieth century the voices of those who claim that the theater is not only dying but actually dead and just doesn't know it yet are particularly strident and, to some ears, persuasive, so that a single playwright's moans may seem just that more poignant and urgent than in Shakespeare's day or in Ibsen's.

Significantly, none of those voices belongs to a working playwright. Our moans are pretty small potatoes by comparison. They're saying the party's over; we're saying give us the opportunity and we'll show you it's just begun. A lot of very good plays are being written right now. They're being produced; they're even being published. The only thing they're not is easier to write.

Very few of them are being produced on Broadway, however, which has led to the false conclusion that they aren't being written at all. Not true. The American theater has never been healthier. It's Broadway that's sick. The American theater is no longer Broadway. It is Los Angeles, it is Seattle, it is Louisville, it is everywhere but the west side of midtown Manhattan.

Just look around. For the first time in our history, we have a *national* theater—regional theaters are in the vanguard of producing the world premieres of our best playwrights. Twenty-five years ago regional theaters produced New York's hits, period.

Now New York is host to the best work of the not-for-profit regional theater.

I was recently asked to appear on a panel saluting "The Golden Age of Gay Theatre." Nonsense. This is a golden age for the American theater, gay *and* straight. The good new plays are being written and produced as I write this introduction. Take it from someone who toils in the trenches: the energy being generated by American playwrights, directors, actors and designers is seismic. With a little luck you'll be reading about them and seeing them and reading them by this time next year. With no luck at all you'll be aware of them in two or three or maybe five years, but I promise you, they're coming soon to a theater near you. The American theater is on a roll, and there is no stopping us.

I wouldn't be a playwright today if it weren't for the regional theater. My regional theater is the Manhattan Theatre Club. I'm a regional theater playwright who just happens to live in New York.

Without the unconditional love of MTC (*support* seems too meager a word), these two plays would never have been written. Knowing that they are committed to me as a writer and not as a playwright who is expected to provide them with "hits" has given me the confidence to write each play as I wanted, not what I think *they* wanted based on expectations from the last play. Thanks to MTC I don't have to compete with myself. There was never any danger that I would be tempted to write *Lips Together, Teeth Apart 2* or *Frankie and Johnny Go to Paris* or *Revenge of the Lisbon Traviata*.

And while I write and dream my next play, I know that I will have a production of it at MTC regardless of its likelihood to succeed with audiences and critics. I may be the only playwright in America who has such an arrangement with a producing theater. Because of it, I know I am the luckiest. I owe Lynne Meadow, Barry Grove and Michael Bush my artistic life. In a profession strewn with too many orphans, they have given me a home that in truth feels more like a fairy tale palace. I have a theater!

Good fortune has allowed me to work with the best actors, directors and designers of these times. The two plays in hand were no exception.

A Perfect Ganesh was inspired by a chance meeting with two American women on a train in India. I knew I would write a play about them one day. But first I had to know who they were and why they had come there. I had to make them "mine," in other words. I came home from India and promptly wrote *Frankie and Johnny in the Clair de Lune*. Next came *The Lisbon Traviata* and *Lips Together, Teeth Apart*. It was only then that I knew who those two women were and what their play would be about.

I wrote the role of Katharine Brynne for the legendary Zoe Caldwell, never daring to hope that she would actually be in it. I had been in awe of her ever since my first trip to England in 1959 and saw her indelible Helena in *All's Well That Ends Well* at Stratford. It was the sort of performance that made you want to have a life in the theater, or else.

I wrote the role of Ganesha for Dominic Cuskern, who at the time was about as universally unknown as an actor as Zoe was everywhere famous. I thought he was a wonderful actor and I knew that he could play a divinity without getting all pretentious and mawkish on us. I was right. He did and triumphed. I like to think I have good taste in actors.

Frances Sternhagen is the kind of flawless actress that any playwright would want to honor his work. Zoe calls her "perfect," and I would agree. Fisher Stevens was astonishing in his many transformations throughout the evening. Now, he told me, I owe him a full-length part. I look forward to it with relish. The man is a joy.

My long-time collaborator John Tillinger directed a perfect production that mirrored the spare eloquence of Ming Cho Lee's perfect set.

Love! Valour! Compassion! had no such specific moment of inspiration as *Ganesh*. The title comes from an entry in John Cheever's journals. I think I wanted to write about what it's like to be a gay man at this particular moment in our history. I think I wanted to tell my friends how much they've meant to me. I think I wanted to tell everyone else who we are when they aren't around. I think I wanted to reach out and let more people into those places in my heart where I don't ordinarily welcome strangers. I think a lot of things about this play, but mainly I think it's much too soon to know what they are. These things take time.

I know for certain, however, that the play was given a definitive production by Joe Mantello and seven remarkable actors: Nathan Lane, Stephen Spinella, John Glover, Stephen Bogardus, John Benjamin Hickey, Justin Kirk and Randy Becker. Loy Arcenas took an impossible design situation and made it seem as easy as it was inevitable.

Manhattan Theatre Club had done it again for me. No wonder I have never been tempted, not once, in all these years, to roam. I like to think I'm smart, too.

So once again I am wallowing in some kind of playwright's heaven. If I'm not careful, I'll forget to moan. This book should have come out months ago. The *Love! Valour! Compassion!* cast hasn't been signed to life-indenturing contracts. The theater was too cold last night. The night before, it was too hot. There, that feels much better. The truth is, I'm worrying about the next play. Will it be any good? What's really scary is that Manhattan Theatre Club will produce it all the same. I have no one to blame if it fails but me. That's terrifying.

Moaning is easier.

—TERRENCE McNALLY
New York City
January 15, 1995

Love! Valour! Compassion!

and

A Perfect Ganesh

Love! Valour! Compassion!

THE PLAYERS

BOBBY BRAHMS, early twenties
RAMON FORNOS, early twenties
BUZZ HAUSER, mid-thirties
JOHN JECKYLL, late forties
JAMES JECKYLL, his twin
GREGORY MITCHELL, early forties
ARTHUR PAPE, late thirties–early forties
PERRY SELLARS, late thirties–early forties

THE SETTING

A remote house and wooded grounds by a lake in Dutchess County, two hours north of New York City.

THE TIME

The present. Memorial Day, Fourth of July, and Labor Day weekends, respectively.

Love! Valour! Compassion! was originally performed at the Manhattan Theatre Club in New York City. It opened November 1, 1994. It was directed by Joe Mantello, with scenery designed by Loy Arcenas; costumes by Jess Goldstein; lighting by Brian MacDevitt; sound by John Kilgore; and choreography by John Carrafa. The production stage manager was William Joseph Barnes. The stage manager was Ira Mont.

THE CAST
(in order of appearance)

GREGORY MITCHELL	Stephen Bogardus
ARTHUR PAPE	John Benjamin Hickey
PERRY SELLARS	Stephen Spinella
JOHN JECKYLL	John Glover
BUZZ HAUSER	Nathan Lane
BOBBY BRAHMS	Justin Kirk
RAMON FORNOS	Randy Becker
JAMES JECKYLL	John Glover

The production subsequently transferred to Broadway where it opened at the Walter Kerr Theatre on January 20, 1995. The only cast change was the role of Perry Sellars, played by Anthony Heald.

For Nathan Lane

Great heart
Great soul
Great actor
Best friend

Bare stage.

There are invisible doors and traps in the walls and floor.

Lights up.

The seven actors are singing "Beautiful Dreamer" by Stephen Foster to a piano accompaniment.

GREGORY *turns out and addresses us.*

GREGORY: Um. I love my. Um. House. Everybody does. I like to fill it with my friends. Um. And walk around the grounds at night and watch them. Um. Through the lighted windows. It makes me happy to see them inside. Um. Our home. Mine. Um. And Bobby's. Um. I'm sorry. Um. I don't do this. Um. On purpose. Um.

ARTHUR: It's okay, Gregory.

GREGORY: It was built in 1915 and still has most of the. Um. Original roof. The wallpaper in the dining room. Um. Is original, too. So is. Um. A lot of the cabinet work. You'd have to be a fool. Um. To change it. This sofa is my pride. Um. And joy. It came with the house. It's genuine. Um. Horsehair. It's itchy but I don't care. I love it.

PERRY: Tell them about the sled.

GREGORY: Jerome Robbins gave me this sled.

PERRY: Mutual admiration, he said. One master choreographer to another.

GREGORY: It's flat here, I said. No hills. Um. What am I going to do with a sled? It's not a sled, Gregory, he told me. It's an antique.

JOHN: It's not an antique, Gregory. It's a piece of junk.

GREGORY: I hope you. Um. Appreciate detail. That. Um. Wainscoting there. This finial here. The main stairs. Um. Have a very gentle rise. Everyone comments how easy it is to. Um. Climb them.

BUZZ: I love your stairs, Gregory. They're so easy.

ARTHUR: Don't tease him like that.

BUZZ: Who's teasing? I wasn't teasing!

GREGORY: They don't build houses like this anymore. Um. The golden age. Um. Of American house building.

BUZZ: If this is going to be Pick On Buzz weekend . . . !

GREGORY: Not architecture, mind you, but house building. This house. Um. Was meant. Um. To stand. Welcome. Make yourself at home.

(*As the men begin to break apart and drift to their various bedrooms, we see that two of them are kissing furiously:* BOBBY *and* RAMON.)

BOBBY: No. No. No.

(*They continue. Now it is* PERRY *who turns to us.*)

PERRY: Anyway. Bobby had gone downstairs for cookies, Pepperidge Farm Brussels, and a glass of milk. Whether Ramon had followed him or was waiting for him, quiet like a cat, bare feet cold on the bare wood floors, I don't know. I was upstairs, asleep with my Arthur.

BUZZ: I was upstairs, asleep with myself. All this I heard later that summer—when everything changed, for good and bad but forever—but I wouldn't have been surprised.

BOBBY: Don't. Stop. Please.

(*They continue.*)

PERRY: Anyway. I prefer the latter: the waiting. It implies certainty. That Bobby would wake up and steal from Gregory's bed and make his way down to their country kitchen—

BUZZ: Which actually was in the country. You're in Dutchess County, two hours north of the city.

PERRY: —and feel unfamiliar arms surround his bare chest from behind, raking his nipples, and in his surprise drop the milk bottle and break it—

(*Sound of a bottle of milk breaking.*)

GREGORY: Bobby?

PERRY: —splattering milk and shards of glass everywhere—

(*A pool of spilt milk is forming around them.*)

ARTHUR: What was that?

PERRY: —pinning them to that spot where they found themselves in the dull light of the still-open Frigidaire door.

(JOHN *sits up in bed.*)

JOHN: Ramon?

BOBBY: Just tell me, who is this?

(RAMON *whispers in his ear.*)

PERRY: What name did Ramon whisper in Bobby's ear that first night? His? One of the others'? Mine?

(*One by one the other four men resume singing.*)

PERRY: Anyway. They stood like this for quite some time and achieved some sort of satisfaction. After he'd come, Ramon whispered more words of love and passion into Bobby's ear, and stole quietly back up the stairs and into the bed he was sharing with John.

JOHN: Where were you?

RAMON: I couldn't sleep.

PERRY: Bobby cleaned up the mess on the kitchen floor, the whole time wondering what an episode like this meant, if, indeed, it meant anything at all.

(ARTHUR *has come into the kitchen area.*)

ARTHUR: What happened?

BOBBY: Perry?

PERRY: That's me.

ARTHUR: It's Arthur.

PERRY: Arthur's my lover. We're often—

ARTHUR: What happened?

PERRY: It's very annoying.

BOBBY: Be careful. There might be broken glass.

ARTHUR: I'm okay, I'm wearing slippers.

PERRY: Arthur is always wearing slippers.

BOBBY: I think I got it all. Did I?

ARTHUR: I can't tell.

PERRY: Bobby is blind.

ARTHUR: Do you mind if I turn the light on? I'm sorry.

BOBBY: It's all right.

PERRY: People are always saying things like that to him. Me, too, and I've known him since he and Gregory got together. Bobby doesn't seem to mind. He has a remarkably loving nature.

ARTHUR: You know the refrigerator door is open?

BOBBY: Thanks. I was just going up. That's all we needed: a refrigerator filled with spoiled food and a houseful of guests.

PERRY: See what I mean? Never puts himself first. I don't understand people like that.

ARTHUR: You're not going anywhere. Sit.

BOBBY: What's the matter?

ARTHUR: You cut yourself. Hang on, I'll be right back.

BOBBY: I'm fine.

ARTHUR: Sit.

(ARTHUR *turns his back to* BOBBY. *We hear running water and the sound of a piece of cloth being torn to make a bandage.*)

I read an article that said most blind people hated to be helped.

BOBBY: We love to be helped. We hate to be patronized. It's people assuming we want help that pisses us off. I'm standing at a corner waiting for the light to change and some jerk grabs my elbow and says, "Don't worry, I've got you." It happens all the time. People think blindness is the most awful thing that can happen to a person. Hey, I've got news for everybody: it's not.

PERRY: I'm not in this conversation. I'm upstairs sleeping in the spoon position with my Arthur. Well, thinking I'm sleeping in the spoon position with my Arthur. Arthur's down in the kitchen expressing his remarkably loving nature to Bobby.

(PERRY *goes to his and Arthur's bed. He hugs a pillow and tries to sleep.*)

BOBBY: "Really, I'm fine," I said.

PERRY: I would have taken him at his word. When someone tells me he's fine, I believe him. But now we're getting Arthur's Mother Teresa.

GREGORY: Don't make yourself sound so cynical, Perry.

PERRY: That's Gregory expressing his remarkably loving nature. Shut up and go back to sleep. It was nothing.

(GREGORY *rolls over.*)

JOHN: Americans confuse sentimentality with love.

PERRY: That's John, expressing his fundamentally hateful one.

(JOHN *is standing with his back to us. We hear the sound of him relieving himself as he turns over his shoulder and addresses* PERRY, *who is trying to sleep.*)

JOHN: It's true, duck.

(ARTHUR *turns around.*)

ARTHUR: I'll try not to hurt.

(*He kneels and begins to dress* BOBBY*'s foot.* ARTHUR *is attracted to* BOBBY.)

BOBBY: Ow!

ARTHUR: Sorry.

PERRY: John is sour. He wrote a musical once. No one liked it. There or here. I don't know why they brought it over.

JOHN: Retaliation for losing the War of Independence.

(*He follows* RAMON.)

PERRY: He's usually funnier than that.

JOHN: I missed you. I said I missed you.

RAMON: I heard you. Ssshh. Go back to sleep.

JOHN: *Te quiero, Ramon Fornos. Te quiero.*

PERRY: Does everyone know what that means? "I love you, Ramon Fornos. I love you."
　　　Anyway, the show closed, John stayed.

JOHN: Some people liked it. Some people rather liked it a lot,
in fact. Not many, but some. The good people.

RAMON: Hey, c'mon, it's late!

PERRY: He's Gregory's rehearsal pianist now. When he's not
pounding out *The Rite of Spring* for Gregory's dancers, he's
working on a new musical-theater project for himself.

JOHN: The life of Houdini. It's got endless possibilities. I've
written thirteen songs.

PERRY: John is always working on a new musical-theater project,
I should hasten to add.

JOHN: What do you mean, you "should hasten to add"? Is that
a crack?

RAMON: I'm going to find another bed if you keep this up.

PERRY: Anyway!

BUZZ (*stirring*): Did somebody say something about musicals?
I distinctly heard something about musicals. Somebody
somewhere is talking about musicals!

(*He sits up with a start.* PERRY *holds him.*)

I was having a musical comedy nightmare. They were going to revive *The King and I* for Tommy Tune and Elaine Stritch. We've got to stop them!

PERRY: Buzz liked John's musical.

BUZZ: It had a lot of good things in it.

PERRY: Buzz likes musicals, period.

BUZZ: I'm just a Gershwin with a Romberg rising in the house of Kern.

PERRY (*to us*): He's off.

BUZZ: I was conceived after a performance of *Wildcat* with Lucille Ball. I don't just love Lucy, I owe my very existence to her. For those of you who care but don't know, *Wildcat* was a musical by Cy Coleman and Carolyn Leigh with a book by N. Richard Nash. It opened December 16, 1960, at the Alvin Theatre and played for 172 performances. Two of its most-remembered songs are "Hey, Look Me Over!" and "Give a Little Whistle." For those of you who care but know all that, I'm sorry. For those of you who don't know and don't care, I'm really sorry. You're going to have a lot of trouble with me.

So what's up, doc?

PERRY: Buzz, you weren't awake for this.

BUZZ: If I was, I don't remember it.

PERRY: You weren't.

BUZZ: Okay. (*He rolls over and goes back to sleep.*)

PERRY: If it isn't about musicals, Buzz has the attention span of a very small moth. That wasn't fair. Buzz isn't well. He makes costumes for Gregory's company and does volunteer work at an AIDS clinic in Chelsea. He says he's going to find the cure for this disease all by himself and save the world for love and laughter.

BUZZ: It sounds ridiculous when you say it like that!

PERRY: I know. I'm sorry.

(*He kisses* BUZZ *on the head, goes back to his own bed, picks up a pillow, and hugs it close to him.*)

None of us were awake for this.

(*Gentle snoring begins—or humming, maybe.*)

(ARTHUR *has stopped bandaging* BOBBY*'s foot. He is just looking at him now. His hand goes out and would touch* BOBBY*'s bare chest or arms or legs, but doesn't.*)

BOBBY: What are you doing?

ARTHUR: I guess you should know: there's a rather obvious stain on your pajamas.

BOBBY: Thanks.

ARTHUR: I didn't know I could still blush at my age.

BOBBY: That's okay. Your secret is safe with me.

ARTHUR: So is yours.

BOBBY: I'm the one who should be blushing, only blind men don't blush.

ARTHUR: That sounds like the title of one of Perry's detective novels.

BOBBY: I had sort of an accident.

ARTHUR: What you had was a mortal sin. I hope you both did. You know what we used to call them back in Catholic boys' school? Nocturnal emissions. It's so much nicer than "wet dream." It always made me think of Chopin. Nocturnal Emission in C-sharp Minor.

BOBBY: I don't want Greg to know.

ARTHUR: I swear to God, I only came down here for a glass of milk.

BOBBY: I swear to God, I did, too.

ARTHUR: We don't have to have this conversation at three a.m. We don't have to have this conversation ever.

BOBBY: Okay.

ARTHUR: We can talk about you and Greg. We can talk about me and Perry. We can talk about John and his new friend. We could even go back to bed.

BOBBY: It was Ramon.

ARTHUR: I figured.

BOBBY: Why?

ARTHUR: Who else would it be?

BOBBY: I shouldn't have. I'm not very strong that way.

ARTHUR: Most people aren't.

(*They start walking up the stairs to their bedrooms.*)

BOBBY: Is he attractive?

ARTHUR: I'm not supposed to notice things like that. I'm in a relationship.

BOBBY: So am I. Is he?

ARTHUR: I think the word is "hot," Bobby. Okay?
I love these stairs. They're so easy.

BOBBY: Everyone says that.
Have you ever . . . ? On Perry . . . ?

ARTHUR: Yes. I don't recommend it.

BOBBY: Did he find out?

ARTHUR: No, I told him and it's never been the same. It's terrific, but it's not the same.

Here we are. End of the line.

(*He looks at* BOBBY.)

Don't fuck up. You are so . . .

(*He hugs* BOBBY.)

He's not that hot, Bobby. No one is.

BOBBY: I know. Thanks. Goodnight.

(*He goes into* GREGORY'S *room.* GREGORY *is awake.* ARTHUR *joins* PERRY *in their room.* PERRY *is still clutching his pillow.*)

GREGORY: Are you all right?

BOBBY: Ssshh. Go to sleep.

ARTHUR: Sorry.

(*He lies next to* PERRY.)

GREGORY: Where were you?

ARTHUR: Bobby cut himself.

BOBBY: Downstairs.

ARTHUR: He dropped a milk bottle.

BOBBY: I cut myself.

ARTHUR: Remember milk bottles?

BOBBY: I dropped a milk bottle.

(*He lies next to* GREGORY.)

ARTHUR: Only Gregory would have milk bottles.

GREGORY: Are you—?

BOBBY: I'm fine. Arthur took care of me. Go to sleep.

ARTHUR: Are you awake?

GREGORY: I missed you.

(BOBBY *snuggles against* GREGORY.)

BOBBY: Ssshh.

(ARTHUR *rolls over, his back to* PERRY *now.* BUZZ *and* RAMON *are snoring.*)

ARTHUR: He is so young, Perry!

GREGORY: I had a dream. We were in Aspen. The company. We were doing *Wesendonck Lieder.*

ARTHUR: I wanted to hold him.

GREGORY: The record got stuck during ''Der Engel.''

(*Music starts.*)

I had to do it over and over and over.

ARTHUR: Desire is a terrible thing. I'm sorry we're not young anymore.

(GREGORY *begins to sing: very softly, not well, and never fully awake.*)

GREGORY:

In der Kindheit frühen Tagen
Hört'ich oft von Engeln sagen,

(JOHN *sits up, while* RAMON *sleeps beside him, and listens.*)

(GREGORY *is beginning to drift off. At the same time we will hear a soprano singing the same words, her voice gently accompanying his.*)

die des Himmels hehre Wonne,
tauschen mit der Erdensonne . . .

(GREGORY *sleeps. He and* BOBBY *roll over in each other's arms.*
JOHN *has left* RAMON *and come out of their room. The soprano
continues.*)

(*All the men are snoring now.*)

JOHN: I am that merry wanderer of the night. Curiosity, a strange
house, an unfaithful bedfellow drive me. Oh, there are other
distractions, too, of course. A dog barking in the distance.
Bed springs creaking; perhaps love is being made on the
premises. The drip of the toilet on the third floor. Can they
not hear it? But it's mainly the curiosity. I am obsessed
with who people really are. They don't tell us, so I must
know their secrets.

(BUZZ *moans in his sleep.*)

I see things I shouldn't: Buzz is sleeping in a pool of sweat.
They've increased his medication again. And for what?
He's dead.

(*He puts his hand on* BUZZ'*s shoulder, then moves to where*
PERRY *and* ARTHUR *are sleeping.*)

Arthur has begun to sleep with his back to Perry, who
clutches a pillow instead. I overhear what was better left
unsaid: Arthur's sad confession of inappropriate desire. I
read words I often wish were never written. Words that
other eyes were never meant to see.

(*He moves to where* GREGORY *and* BOBBY *are sleeping, takes
up a journal, and reads.*)

"Memorial Day Weekend. Manderley. Out here alone to
work on the new piece. We've invited a full house and
they're predicting rain. We'll see if Fred Avens has fixed
that leak on the north side porch this time. Thought he
would never get around to taking down the storm windows
and putting up the screens. The garden is late. Only the

cukes will be ready. Everything else will have to come from the A&P.'' This isn't quite what I had in mind.

(BUZZ *appears. He is carrying a knapsack.*)

BUZZ: Where is everybody?

JOHN: Did you know Gregory has only three places he feels safe? His work, in Bobby's arms, and in his journal.

BUZZ: That's disgusting.

JOHN: What is? The weather? Or the startling unoriginality of naming your house Manderley, after a kitsch-classic movie?

BUZZ: Reading someone's journal.

JOHN: Did you just get here?

BUZZ: Yes. Where's Gregory?

JOHN: Down by the lake. Are you alone?

BUZZ: No, I have Michael J. Fox in here. Are you?

JOHN: No. "I've rounded up. Um. The usual suspects. Um."

BUZZ: That's not funny. You're a guest in his home.

JOHN: "I think I'll make my special ginger soy vegetable loaf Sunday night." You see why I do this? Gregory's cooking. There's still time to buy steaks.

BUZZ: If I thought you'd ever read anything I wrote when we were together, I'd kill you. I mean it.

JOHN: "I'm stuck on the new piece. Maybe the Webern was a bad choice of music."

BUZZ: I hate what you're doing.

(*He grabs the journal from John.*)

JOHN: I'm puzzled. What kind of statement about his work do you think a choreographer is making by living with a blind person?

BUZZ: I don't know and I don't care. It's not a statement. It's a relationship. Remember them?

JOHN: Nevertheless, the one can't see what the other does. Gregory's work is the deepest expression of who he is—or so one would hope—and Bobby's never seen it.

BUZZ: That's their business. At least they've got someone.

JOHN: Speak for yourself.

BUZZ: So you got lucky this weekend. Don't rub it in. Who is he? Anyone I know?

JOHN: I doubt it.

BUZZ: Is he cute?

JOHN: Yes.

BUZZ: I hate you. I really hate you. What does he do?

JOHN: He's a dancer.

BUZZ: How long have you been seeing him?

JOHN: Three weeks.

BUZZ: Is it serious?

JOHN: In three weeks?

BUZZ: I get serious in about three seconds. People say "What's your rush?" I say, "What's your delay?"

JOHN: What happened to you and—?

BUZZ: I got too intense for him. That's my problem with people. I'm too intense for them. I need someone like Dennis Hopper. A cute, young, gay Dennis Hopper. In the meantime, I'm through with love and all it meant to me.

JOHN: Are you going to be holding that when they come back?

(BUZZ *hasn't resisted stealing a glance at Gregory's journal.*)

BUZZ: Perry's work for Greg is pro bono?

JOHN: Arts advocacy is very in.

BUZZ: He does the clinic, too.

JOHN: So is AIDS. I'm sorry.

BUZZ: That's five dollars. Anyone who mentions AIDS this summer, it'll cost them.

JOHN: Who made this rule up?

BUZZ: I did. It's for the kitty. Cough it up.

(JOHN *holds his hand out for the journal.*)

BUZZ: Did you?

JOHN: Did I what?

BUZZ: Ever read anything I wrote?

JOHN: I don't know. Probably. I don't remember. If you left it out, yes.

BUZZ: I would hardly call a journal left on someone's desk in their own room in their own home while they took the other guests swimming ''out.''

(*He returns the journal.*)

JOHN: People who keep journals—thank you—expect them to be read by people like me. They just pretend they don't. Freud was on to them like that!

(*He snaps his fingers while continuing to skim the pages of the journal.*)

(*We hear thunder. It will increase.*)

BUZZ: Shit, it's going to rain.

JOHN: Here's something about you.

BUZZ: I don't want to hear it.

JOHN: "It's Buzz's birthday. We got him an out-of-print record-ing of an obscure musical called *Seventeen*."

BUZZ: I have *Seventeen*.

JOHN: "They assured us he wouldn't have it."

BUZZ: Don't worry, I'll act surprised.

JOHN: "It cost seventy-five dollars." You better act more than surprised.

BUZZ: I just paid a hundred and a quarter for it. They said it was the last copy.

JOHN: Calm down. You can exchange it.

BUZZ: For what? *CALL ME MADAM*? I mean, how many copies of a forgotten musical that opened in 1951 and ran 182 performances at the Broadhurst Theatre are they going to sell in one week? Do you know what the odds are against this sort of thing? This is like the time Tim Sheahan and Claude Meade both got me *Whoop-Up*!

(JOHN *has resumed reading in the journal, but* BUZZ *continues, speaking to us.*)

You may wonder why I fill my head with such trivial-seem-ing information. First of all, it isn't trivial to me, and sec-ond, I can contain the world of the Broadway musical. Get my hands around it, so to speak. Be the master of one little universe. Besides, when I'm alone, it gives me great plea-sure to sing and dance around the apartment. I especially like "Big Spender" from *Sweet Charity* and "I'm Going Back Where I Can Be Me" from *Bells Are Ringing*. I could never do this with anyone watching, of course. Even a boy-friend, if I had one, which I don't. I'd be too inhibited.

So, when I'm not at the clinic thinking I am single-handedly going to find the cure for this fucking scourge (it doesn't sound ridiculous when I say it, not to me!), I am to be found at my place in Chelsea doing "Rose's Turn" from *GYPSY*.

I can't think of the last time I didn't cry myself to sleep.

Hey, it's no skin off your nose.

I think that is so loathsome of you, John.

(GREGORY *and* RAMON *return from swimming.*)

GREGORY: Hello! We're back! Where is. Um. Everybody?

JOHN: I'd better return this.

BUZZ: We're up here.

GREGORY: John?

JOHN: Coming.

GREGORY: You don't know. Um. What you're missing. The lake is. Um. Wonderful.

RAMON: Don't believe him. It's freezing! (*He drops his towel.*) *¡Ay! ¡Coño! ¡Madre de Dios!*

GREGORY: Did. Um. The others get here?

JOHN: Just Buzz!

BUZZ: Hello.

GREGORY: Buzz!

RAMON: My nuts. Where are they? I have no nuts. They're gone.

GREGORY: They're not gone. Um. They're just. Um. Hiding.

(JOHN *and* BUZZ *have returned.*)

RAMON: I had enormous nuts. I was famous for my nuts. Where are my fabulous nuts?

JOHN: I warned you, sweetheart. They got so cold in Gregory's lake they fell off and one of those goddamn snapping turtles is eating them as we speak.

GREGORY: My turtles don't. Um. Snap, Ramon. This is Buzz.

RAMON: Hi, Buzz. I had balls. He doesn't believe me. Tell him about my balls, John.

JOHN: Ramon had legendary balls up until twenty minutes ago.

BUZZ: I know. I've been following them for the last two seasons. From a tiny performance space in the East Village all the way to the Opera House at BAM. The three of you have come a long way, baby.

JOHN: Do you believe this man and I were an item?

BUZZ: A wee item, Ramon.

JOHN: You don't want to go there, Buzz.

BUZZ: But seriously (and don't you hate people who begin sentences "But seriously"?), are you guys going to be back at the Joyce? That last piece was sensational.

GREGORY: You mean *Verklärte Nacht*?

BUZZ: Speak English! The man can barely get a whole sentence out and then he hits us with *Verklärte Nacht!* (*Then to* RAMON:) I don't suppose you want to get married?

RAMON: No, but thank you.

BUZZ: Just thought I'd get it out there. Anyway, *Verklärte Schmatta*, whatever it is, was a thrilling piece. It blew me away. And you were fantastic.

RAMON: Thank you.

BUZZ: Your balls weren't bad, either. I stood.

GREGORY: It was wonderful work. Wonderful. Um. Energy.

RAMON: You saw us, Mr. Mitchell?

GREGORY: I wanted to know. Um. What all the. Um. Shouting was about.

RAMON: I would have freaked if I'd known you were out there, Mr. Mitchell.

GREGORY: It's Gregory, please. You're making me feel. Um. Like. Um. An old man with "Mr. Mitchell." It was great. You reminded me. Um. Of me. Um. At your age.

BUZZ: "So what's next for you guys?" he asked in a casual, bantering voice, though his heart was beating so hard he was sure everyone could hear it.

RAMON: Right now we're all just hoping there will be a next season. We're broke.

GREGORY: Every company is, Ramon.

RAMON: Not yours, surely.

BUZZ: It's "Gregory." He doesn't like "Shirley." I'm sorry. Ignore me.

JOHN: He is.

BUZZ: What you people need is a Diaghilev.

RAMON: What's a Diaghilev?

BUZZ: A rich older man who in return for certain favors funds an entire ballet company.

RAMON: Where is this rich older dude? I'm all his.

JOHN: Don't you want to know what these favors are first?

RAMON: I'm a big boy. I have a pretty good idea.

GREGORY: I'm in line first for him, Ramon.

BUZZ: Gregory, your dancers love you. We all do. We'd work for you for free.

GREGORY: I won't let you. Artists should be paid.

RAMON: Right on. The only thing an artist should do for free is make love.

JOHN: Now you tell me. Now he tells me! This is getting entirely too artsy-fartsy/idealistic/intellectual for me. Can we go upstairs and fuck?

GREGORY: I'm going to start. Um. Dinner. They should be here soon. I thought. Um. I'd make my special. Um. *Penne Primavera.*

(*He goes.*)

BUZZ: I brought those sketches you wanted. I've got everyone in Lycra. Lots and lots of Lycra. I'm entering my Lycra period.
　　　You still know how to clear a room, John.

(*He goes.*)

RAMON: I didn't appreciate that fucking remark in front of your friends.

JOHN: I don't appreciate you flapping your dick in everybody's face, okay? Are you coming upstairs?

RAMON: Maybe.

(JOHN *heads upstairs.*)

(GREGORY *looks at his watch and begins to chop onions.*)

(BUZZ *covers his eyes with some computer printouts and rests.*)

(JOHN *waits upstairs while* RAMON *sits downstairs.*)

(ARTHUR, PERRY, *and* BOBBY *come into view. They are driving in heavy traffic.*)

PERRY: Cunt! Goddamn cunt! Fuck you and your ultimate driving machine!

ARTHUR: Perry!

PERRY: Well, they *are* when they drive like that.

ARTHUR: Don't use that word.

PERRY: Men are cunts when they drive like that. Did you see how she just cut right in front of me?

BOBBY: Are you talking to me? Sorry, I was reading the life of Ray Charles. What happened?

PERRY: Some asshole-whore-cunt-bitch-dyke with New Jersey license plates and Republican candidates on her bumper practically took my fender off at seventy miles an hour.

BOBBY: It sounds like an extremely cuntlike maneuver, Batman.

PERRY: You see? Boy Wonder agree with Bruce.

ARTHUR: I think you're both disgusting. If I had any convictions I'd ask you to let me out right here.

PERRY: You have too many convictions. That's your trouble.

ARTHUR: Maybe you have too few and that's yours.

PERRY: They're just words. They don't mean anything.

ARTHUR: Can I quote him, Batboy?

PERRY: I was mad. Words only mean something if you say them when you're not mad and mean them. I agree: "Nancy Reagan is a cunt" is an offensive remark.

BOBBY: I wouldn't go that far, Bruce.

PERRY: But "Cunt!" when she grabs a cab in front of you after you've been waiting twenty minutes on a rainy night and she just pops out from Lutèce is a justifiable emotional response to an enormous social injustice.

BOBBY: You're right. He's right. Let's all kill ourselves.

ARTHUR: All I'm saying is, it's never right to use words to hurt another person.

PERRY: How did I hurt her? She didn't hear me. She's halfway to Poughkeepsie by now, the bitch. Don't get me started again. I was just calming down.

ARTHUR: We hurt ourselves when we use them. We're all diminished.

PERRY: You're right. I don't agree with you, but you're right.

ARTHUR: Of course I'm right, you big fairy. And what are you laughing at back there, you visual gimp? There's no really good insulting word for a blind person, is there?

BOBBY: I think you people decided nature had done enough to us and declared a moratorium.

PERRY: Do you ever wonder what Gregory looks like?

ARTHUR: Perry!

BOBBY: It's all right. I don't mind. I know what he looks like.

PERRY: No, I mean, what he really looks like.

BOBBY: I know what he really looks like. He's handsome. His eyes shine. He has wonderful blond hair.

PERRY: But you've never seen blond hair. You have no concept of it.

BOBBY: In my mind's eye, I do, Horatio.

ARTHUR: That shut you up.

BOBBY: That wasn't my intention. In my mind's eye, I see very clearly the same things you and Perry take for granted. Gregory's heart is beautiful.

PERRY: What do we look like?

ARTHUR: Perry!

BOBBY: Like bookends.

PERRY: Is that a compliment?

BOBBY: I think you've come to look more and more like each other over the years.

PERRY: You haven't known us that long.

ARTHUR: That's not what he's saying.

BOBBY: I think you love each other very much. I think you'll stick it out, whatever. I think right now you're holding hands—that when Perry has to take his hand from yours, Arthur, to steer in traffic, he puts it back in yours as soon as he can. I think this is how you always drive. I think this is how you go through life.

ARTHUR: Don't stop.

BOBBY: I think you're both wearing light blue Calvin Klein shirts and chinos.

PERRY: Wrong!

ARTHUR: Look out for that car—!

PERRY: I see it, I see it! What color is my hair?

BOBBY: What hair? You're totally bald.

PERRY: Wrong again. What color?

BOBBY: I wanted to be wrong. I don't like this game. It's making me afraid.

RAMON: Okay.

(*He stands up.*)

JOHN: He's coming.

(RAMON *starts up to John's room.*)

PERRY: I'm sorry. I didn't . . .

(*They drive in silence.*)

(RAMON *comes into the bedroom.* JOHN *is sitting on the bed.*)

JOHN: Hello.

RAMON: Hi.

JOHN: I'm sorry.

RAMON: Look, I'm sort of out of my element this weekend. He's Gregory Mitchell, for Christ's sake. Do you know what that means? You're all old friends. You work together. You have a company. I'm just somebody you brought with you. I'd appreciate a little more respect, okay? I'm being honest.

JOHN: Okay.

RAMON: Thank you. What's wrong with your neck?

JOHN: Would you be an angel and massage my shoulders?

RAMON: Sure. Just show me where.

(RAMON *works on* JOHN.)

BOBBY: Now it's my turn. I want you to tell me what someone looks like.

PERRY: Don't tell me, let me guess: Tom Cruise, Willard Scott. I give up, who?

BOBBY: John.

ARTHUR: John Jeckyll?

BOBBY: What does he look like? Describe him. After all this time, I still can't get a picture.

PERRY: Can you visualize Satan, Bobby?

ARTHUR: Don't start.

PERRY: Do you have a concept of evil?

BOBBY: A very good one, actually.

ARTHUR: Not everyone shares your opinion, Perry. Perry has a problem with John, Bobby.

PERRY: I don't have a problem with him. I can't stand him and I wish he were dead.

JOHN: Don't stop.

PERRY: Beware him, Bobby. People like you are too good for this world, so people like John Jeckyll have to destroy them.

ARTHUR: You can't say these things, Perry.

PERRY: Yes, I can. He doesn't have to believe them.

BOBBY: I'm not so good. If anything, this world is too good for us.

PERRY: What do you care what John Jeckyll looks like anyway?

BOBBY: I just wondered. People like that intrigue me.

PERRY: What? Shits?

ARTHUR: It's going to be a wonderful weekend.

PERRY: What does that mean?

ARTHUR: John had nowhere to go, so Gregory invited him.

BOBBY: Didn't Gregory tell you?

PERRY: No, he did not. Probably because he knew I wouldn't come if he did. Shit! Why would Greg do this to me?

ARTHUR: He didn't. He told me. I elected not to tell you.

PERRY: Why?

ARTHUR: "Why?"!

PERRY: I assume he's coming alone.

ARTHUR: Why would you assume that?

PERRY: Who would willingly spend Memorial Day weekend at a wonderful big house in the country on a gorgeous lake with John Jeckyll when they could be suffocating in the city all by themselves?

BOBBY: He's bringing someone.

ARTHUR: A new boyfriend?

PERRY: One of the Menendez brothers.

BOBBY: A dancer.

ARTHUR: Someone from the company?

BOBBY: No. I think Greg said his name was Ramon. Ramon Something.

ARTHUR: Sounds Latino.

PERRY: "Something" sounds Latino? Since when?

BOBBY: He's Puerto Rican.

PERRY: A Third World boyfriend. So John Jeckyll has gone PC.

ARTHUR: I don't think Puerto Rico qualifies as Third World.

PERRY: This is like Adolf Hitler shtupping Anne Frank.

ARTHUR: You are really over the top this afternoon!

PERRY: Wait till the weekend's over! Here's the driveway. You're home, Bobby.

(*Sounds of the car approaching. Everyone in the house reacts to the sound of it.*)

GREGORY: They're here! Buzz, John! They're here! I hear the car!

PERRY: Any other surprises for us, Bobby?

JOHN: I guess they're here. Perry and Arthur are lovers. Bobby is Greg's.

RAMON: I'm terrible with names.

GREGORY: Buzz, wake up, they're here!

BUZZ: I was dreaming about a vacuum cleaner. I need to get laid.

(GREGORY, BUZZ, JOHN, *and* RAMON *go to greet the others, who are carrying bags.*)

GREGORY: I was beginning to. Um. Worry. How was the. Um. Traffic?

PERRY: Terrible. Especially before Hawthorne Circle.

ARTHUR: I told him to take the Thruway, but no!

BUZZ: The train was horrendous. I should have waited for you. But guess who I saw? Tony Leigh and Kyle. Together again. A handshake? What is this shit? I want a hug, Martha.

GREGORY: Where's my. Um. Angel?

BOBBY: Hi. Have you been working?

GREGORY: I didn't leave. Um. The studio. Um. All week.

BOBBY: How did it go?

GREGORY: Great. Don't ask. Terrible.

(*They embrace and withdraw a little.*)

JOHN: Hello, Perry. Arthur. You both look terrific. Don't you two put on weight? Ever? Anywhere?

ARTHUR: Look who's talking! I'd love to see the portrait in his closet.

JOHN: No, you wouldn't. Ramon, Arthur and Perry.

PERRY: He's Arthur, I'm Perry. He's nice, I'm not. Hi.

ARTHUR: We're both nice. Don't listen to him.

BUZZ: So what are you driving now, boys? A Ford Taurus?

PERRY: What do you care, you big fruit? I don't know. I just get in, turn the key, and go. When they stop, I get a new one.

JOHN: You should see the wreck we rented.

ARTHUR: It's a Mazda 626, Buzz.

PERRY: He's so butch.

ARTHUR: Someone had to do it. That's why he married me. Can you change a tire?

PERRY: No.

ARTHUR: Neither can I.

BUZZ: That's from *Annie Get Your Gun.* ''Can you bake a pie?'' ''No.'' ''Neither can I.'' Ethel Merman was gay, you know. So was Irving Berlin. I don't think English is Ramon's first language.

GREGORY: I missed you.

BOBBY: It's so good to be here. The city is awful. You can't breathe. They still haven't fixed the dryer. Flor was in hysterics. Here. I've got your mail in my backpack.

GREGORY: What's this?

BOBBY: The CDs you wanted. And I got your sheet music from Patelson's.

GREGORY: You didn't have to.

BOBBY: I wanted to.

GREGORY: John, look, the Elliott Carter!

RAMON (*to* BOBBY): Hi, I'm Ramon.

GREGORY: I'm sorry!

(RAMON *puts his hand out to* BOBBY.)

Bobby doesn't. Um. See, Ramon.

RAMON: I'm sorry. I didn't—

BOBBY: Don't be sorry. Just come here!

(*He hugs* RAMON.)

Welcome. Ramon, is it?

RAMON: Right.

BOBBY: Latino?

RAMON: Yes.

BOBBY: *Mi casa es su casa.* I bet you were wishing I wasn't going to say that.

BUZZ: We all were, Bobby.

PERRY, ARTHUR, BUZZ: We all were!

RAMON: Listen, that's about as much Spanish as I speak.

BOBBY: You're kidding.

RAMON: Sorry to disappoint you. The Commonwealth of Puerto Rico is a territory of U.S. imperialism.

JOHN: No speeches, please, Ramon. No one's interested.

RAMON: We speak American. We think American. We dress American. The only thing we don't do is move or make love American.

BOBBY: I've been like this since birth, Ramon. Gregory and I have been together four years. I get around fine. It'll surprise you. Any more questions?

RAMON (*off guard*): No.

(*They separate.*)

GREGORY: Let me. Um. Show you. Um. To your room.

ARTHUR: After all these years, I think we know, Gregory. If those walls could talk!

BUZZ: They don't have to. We've all heard you.

ARTHUR: What room are you in?

BUZZ: That little horror under the eaves. I call it the Patty Hearst Memorial Closet.

ARTHUR: Give me a hand with these, will you, Perry?

PERRY: I told you not to take so much.

ARTHUR: It's my hair dryer.

PERRY: You don't have enough hair to justify an appliance that size.

ARTHUR: Has it ever occurred to you that I stopped listening to you at least ten years ago?

RAMON: Here, let me.

ARTHUR: Thank you.

(*They will start moving to the house.*)

GREGORY: We're having. Um. Salade Nicoise. Um. For lunch.

BUZZ: You know I'm allergic to anchovies.

GREGORY: We just. Um. Swam the float out. Me. Um. And Ramon.

BUZZ: He knows I'm allergic to anchovies.

PERRY: I'm not going in that lake until you get it heated.

GREGORY: I hope you brought. Um. Your swimsuits.

ARTHUR: No one is wearing swimsuits. We're all going skinny-dipping after lunch. What are we? Men or wimps?

BUZZ: You just want to see everyone's dick.

ARTHUR: I've seen everyone's dick. Answer the question.

BUZZ: Sometimes we're men and sometimes we're wimps. You haven't seen Ramon's dick.

ARTHUR: You're a troublemaker.

BUZZ: I'm not a troublemaker. I'm an imp. A gay imp.

(*He goes. The new arrivals are beginning to settle in.*)

(PERRY *and* JOHN *remain for the following until indicated.*)

PERRY: Anyway. Gregory knew he'd left Bobby downstairs and outside the house.

GREGORY: Does everyone. Um. Have towels?

PERRY: It was their ritual. Whenever they arrived at the house from the city, Bobby liked to be alone outside for a while, even in winter. Gregory never asked what he did.

BOBBY: Hello, house.

ARTHUR: Greg! We need some towels.

PERRY: No, we don't. We brought our own. Remember?

BOBBY: Hello, trees.

ARTHUR: Never mind! That's right, we hate his towels.

BOBBY: Hello, lake.

GREGORY: Who said they needed towels?

PERRY: Greg's house is very large.

ARTHUR: Too large. I get sick of shouting. We're fine! Forget the towels!

BOBBY: I bless you all.

PERRY: None of us saw Ramon when he returned to the driveway, the parked cars, and Bobby. Arthur and I were settling in.

(RAMON *has returned to where* BOBBY *is standing. He watches him.*)

JOHN: I was on the phone to London with my brother, James.

PERRY: I didn't know you had a brother.

JOHN: A twin brother. We're like *that. (He opens his arms wide.)* He's not well.

PERRY: I'm sorry.

JOHN: This is about them.

(*He nods toward* BOBBY *and* RAMON.)

PERRY: Minutes passed. Gregory fussed. Buzz washed salad greens in his hosts' pricey balsamic vinegar. He's very diligent about germs. He has to be. Ramon looked at Bobby.

BOBBY: Thank you, God.

RAMON: Excuse me?

BOBBY: Who's that?

RAMON: I'm sorry.

BOBBY: You startled me.

RAMON: It's Ramon. I'm sorry. I thought you said something.

BOBBY: I was thanking God for all this. The trees, the lake, the sweet, sweet air. For being here. For all of us together in Gregory's house.

RAMON: I didn't mean to interrupt or anything.

BOBBY: I'm not crazy. I'm happy.

RAMON: I understand.

GREGORY: Here are the towels you asked for.

ARTHUR: Thank you.

GREGORY: Anything else?

ARTHUR: We're fine.

GREGORY: Perry?

PERRY: We're fine.

GREGORY: Um. I'm glad. Um. You're both here.

RAMON: Do you need a hand with anything?

BOBBY: No, thanks.

BUZZ: Pssst! Gregory!

GREGORY: What?

BUZZ: John is on the phone to his brother in London. I didn't
    hear him use a credit card or reverse the charges.

GREGORY: Um. I'm sure he'll. Um. Tell me.

BUZZ: Don't you ever believe the worst about anyone?

GREGORY: No.

(RAMON *hasn't moved. He scarcely breathes. He has not taken
his eyes off* BOBBY.)

BOBBY: You're still there, aren't you? What are you doing? What
    do you want? Don't be afraid. Tell me. All right. Don't.
    Stay there. I'll come to you. Just tell me, should I fall
    (which I don't plan to), what color are my trousers? I think
    I put on white. I hope so. It's Memorial Day.

PERRY: I don't know why, but I'm finding this very painful.

BOBBY: Children play at this and call it Blindman's Bluff. Imagine your whole life being a children's birthday-party game!

JOHN: Painful, erotic, and absurd.

BOBBY: I can feel you. I can hear you. I'm getting warm. I'm getting close. I like this game. I'm very good at it. I'm going to win. You haven't got a chance.

PERRY: Bobby didn't see the rake.

(BOBBY *trips and falls. He hurts himself. There will be a gash on his forehead.*)

RAMON: Oh!

BOBBY: He speaks! The cat has let go his tongue. I wouldn't say no to a hand.

(RAMON *goes.* BOBBY *calls after him.*)

At least tell me, what color are my trousers?

PERRY (*moved*): White. White.

BOBBY: Sometimes I get tired of behaving like a grown-up. Ow! Gregory!

(*At once, everyone converges on the scene and surrounds him.*)

GREGORY: What happened?

BOBBY: I'm okay. Just—

GREGORY: The rake! You tripped. It's my fault. Um.

PERRY: Take his other arm.

BOBBY: I'm fine. I want Gregory to do it.

BUZZ: Who would leave a rake out like that?

ARTHUR: Shut up, will you?

JOHN: He's cut.

BOBBY: I'm not cut.

JOHN: His forehead.

BOBBY: What color are my trousers?

GREGORY: White.

BOBBY: Are there grass stains on them?

BUZZ: Bobby, you are the only fairy in America who still wears white pants on the first holiday of summer.

BOBBY: I was hoping I was the only person in America who still wears white pants on the first holiday of summer.

PERRY: White pants were before my time even, and I'm pushing forty.

BUZZ: Not. You pushed forty when *Chorus Line* was still running.

PERRY: That's not true. I was born in 19—

ARTHUR: We have an injured person here.

(RAMON *returns.*)

BOBBY: I'm not injured.

JOHN: Where have you been?

RAMON: Down by the lake. What happened?

BOBBY: Nothing happened. Who's that?

BUZZ: The new kid on the block.

RAMON: Is he all right?

BOBBY: I fell. Big deal. I do it all the time.

GREGORY: No, you don't. No, he doesn't.

BOBBY: Now everyone back off. Everyone but Gregory. I can feel you all crowding around me.

GREGORY: One!

BOBBY: What are you doing?

BUZZ: Rhett picks up Scarlett and carries her up the stairs.

GREGORY: Two!

BOBBY: No, I don't want you to.

GREGORY: Three!

(*He tries to pick* BOBBY *up but can't. He staggers with the weight, then sets him down. The others look away in embarrassment.*)

I couldn't get a good. Um. Grip.

BOBBY: It's not you. It's all that ice cream I've been eating.

GREGORY: That's never happened. Usually I—I feel so—

BOBBY: It's okay, it's okay.

(BOBBY *and* GREGORY *go into the house. The others hang behind somewhat sheepishly.*)

BUZZ (*singing*): "Just a weekend in the country."

RAMON: Is that a joke?

BUZZ: Come on, I need you in the kitchen. I'll explain the entire Sondheim oeuvre to you while we peel potatoes. I'm borrowing your humpy boyfriend, John. I love the way I said that. Oeuvre. I'm quite impressed. Oeuvre. Say it with me. Oeuvre.

(BUZZ *and* RAMON *go.*)

ARTHUR: Don't ever try to pick me up.

PERRY: It's lucky for you I did.

JOHN: I'd rung off from my brother feeling a rage and a desolation I didn't know how to cope with. "Didn't"? I never have.

ARTHUR: What's the matter?

JOHN: My twin brother. The National Theatre seamstress. He wants to come over. He's not well. He needs me and I don't like him.

ARTHUR: That's a tough order. I don't envy you.
        Perry, I'm going to take a canoe out. You want to come?

PERRY: I promised Greg I'd go over some company business with him.

ARTHUR: It's your last chance to get rid of me.

PERRY: No, it's not.

(ARTHUR *goes. Only* PERRY *and* JOHN *remain.*)

    I work with quite a few AIDS organizations.

JOHN: Thank you.

PERRY: They can help him find a doctor.

JOHN: Thank you.

PERRY: It never ends.

JOHN: No.

PERRY: How does Buzz look to you?

JOHN: I don't know. How does he look to you?

PERRY: I can't tell anymore.

JOHN: He wouldn't tell me if things were worse.

PERRY: I can't look at him sometimes.

JOHN: Anyway.

PERRY (*pleasantly*): You got that from me, you know.

JOHN: Got what?

PERRY: The "anyway."

JOHN: It's a word in the dictionary. Page 249. You can't copy-right the English language, duck.

PERRY: Hey, I'm trying! Fuck you.

(*He goes.*)

JOHN: Anyway. *En tout cas!* The weekend had begun. Everyone was in place. Old wounds reopened. New alliances forged. For fifteen minutes, while I helped Arthur wash their car, he was my best friend in the entire world. Later that afternoon, after too much picnic, when I came upon him and Perry all cozy in a hammock on the porch, he barely gave me the time of day. The hours until dinner seemed endless.

(*The other men are reassembling for after-dinner after a very big meal.*)

PERRY: No, Gregory. It's out of the question. Jesus, I hope this isn't why you invited us out here for the weekend.

GREGORY: I've. Um. Committed us.

PERRY: Well *un*commit us!

GREGORY: It's too late.

PERRY: Leave it to me. I'll get you out of it.

GREGORY: No, I want to. Um. Do it. It's for a good cause.

PERRY: I don't care if it's the greatest cause in the history of Western civilization, which it's not, you are not going to find six men, nondancers all, to put on tutus and do *Swan Lake* for another AIDS benefit at Carnegie Hall. You're not going to find one man!

BUZZ: Speak for yourself, Perry.

PERRY: Well, *you*! The love child of Judy Garland and Liberace.

ARTHUR: When is it, Greg?

GREGORY: Um. It's. Um. Early September, right after Labor Day.

PERRY: Bobby, tell your lover he is not going to find six men to make fools of themselves like that.

BOBBY: How would they be making fools of themselves?

PERRY: By dressing like women. Men in drag turn my stomach.

RAMON: Why?

ARTHUR: Don't start, Perry.

BUZZ: You wouldn't be in drag. I'd have you in tulle, lots and lots of tulle. A vision of hairy legs in a tutu and toe shoes.

PERRY: This will go over big at the NEA, Gregory. That's all we need. A picture of you looking like some flaming fairy in the Arts and Leisure section.

GREGORY: I. Um. I am a flaming fairy. I thought we all were.

PERRY: You know what I'm talking about.

BOBBY: Don't yell at him. It was my idea. I thought it would be funny.

PERRY: What do you know about funny? I'm sorry, Bobby, but sometimes boyfriends should stay boyfriends.

GREGORY: Sometimes. Um. Lawyers should stay. Um. Lawyers.

PERRY: You've done enough for AIDS. We all have.

GREGORY: Nobody's done enough. Um. For AIDS.

BOBBY: It's okay, Gregory.

GREGORY: Never mind, Perry. I'll ask someone else.
Now who wants what?

ARTHUR: We're all fine.

PERRY: No, we're not.

JOHN: People are bloody sick of benefits, Gregory.

PERRY: That's the truth.

BUZZ: Not the people they're being given for.

GREGORY: *Basta*, Buzz. The subject is closed.

ARTHUR: Dinner was delicious. The mashed potatoes were fabulous, Gregory.

BUZZ: The mashed potatoes were mine.

(*He sings from* The King and I.)

I don't know why I've bothered to perfect a flawless imitation of Gertrude Lawrence when none of you cretins has even heard of her!

JOHN: We've heard, love. We don't care.

BOBBY: Who's Gertrude Lawrence?

PERRY: A British actress.

GREGORY: She was. Um. Gay, you know.

BUZZ: That's not funny. Julie Andrews made a rotten film about her.

ARTHUR: Isn't Julie Andrews gay?

BUZZ: I don't know. She never fucked me. Don't interrupt. Gertrude Lawrence wasn't an actress. She was a star. Hence, the rotten film, *Star!*, but don't get me started on movies. Movies are for people who have to eat popcorn while they're being entertained. Next question? Yes, you, at the end of the table with the lindenberry sorbet all over his face.

RAMON: Who's Julie Andrews?

BUZZ: I should have seen that one coming. I was born in the wrong decade, that's my problem.

RAMON: I was kidding. I saw *Mary Poppins*. But who's Liberace?

BOBBY: Who's Judy Garland? Who are any of those people?

(BOBBY *and* RAMON *laugh together.*)

ARTHUR: You want me to clear up, Gregory?

BUZZ: Who's Ethel Merman? Who's Mary Martin? Who's Beatrice Lillie? Who's anybody? We're all going to be dead and forgotten anyway.

BOBBY: Gregory's not.

BUZZ: I'm talking about mattering!

PERRY: I just don't want to be dead and forgotten in my own lifetime.

ARTHUR: Nattering?

BUZZ: Mattering! Really mattering.

ARTHUR: Oh, I thought you said "nattering"!

JOHN: You admit people like Gertrude Lawrence don't really matter?

ARTHUR: I thought he said "nattering."

BUZZ: I cannot believe a subject of the U.K. could make a remark like that. Gertrude Lawrence brought pleasure to hundreds of thousands of people. You wrote a musical that ran for eleven performances.

JOHN: I have United States citizenship.

RAMON: I know who Barbra Streisand is.

BUZZ: She'll be very pleased to hear that.

BOBBY: I don't know who most of those people are, either.

PERRY: When did you take out U.S. citizenship?

JOHN: Nine years ago. October 25.

BUZZ: Barbara Cook's birthday. "Who's Barbara Cook?" No one. Nobody. Forget it. Die listening to your Madonna albums. I long for the day when people ask "Who's Madonna?" I apologize to the teenagers at the table, but the state of the American musical has me very upset.

PERRY: The state of America is what should get you upset.

BUZZ: It does. It's a metaphor, you asshole!

PERRY: Now just a minute!

BUZZ: I have a picture of a starving child in Somalia over my desk at the clinic. He's covered in dust.

JOHN: We all know the picture.

PERRY: It doesn't justify you calling me an asshole.

BUZZ: The child has fallen forward on his haunches, he's so weak from hunger, he can barely lift his head.

PERRY: Buzz, we know the picture. It was in every magazine and paper.

BUZZ: Clearly, the kid is dying. He's got what? Five minutes? Ten? Five feet away a vulture sits. Sits and waits. He's not even looking at the kid. He's that confident where his next meal is coming from. There's no way this kid is going to jump up and launch into a number from *Oliver!* or *Porgy and Bess*.

PERRY: We've all seen the picture!

BOBBY (*quietly*): I haven't.

(GREGORY *takes his hand.*)

PERRY: What is your point?

BUZZ: Point? I don't have a point. Why does everything have to have a point? To make it comfortable? I look at that picture every day and I get sick to my stomach and some days I even cry a little. The newspaper has already yellowed, but the nausea and the occasional tears keep coming. But so what? So fucking what? That kid is dead meat by now.

JOHN: That's disgusting.

BUZZ: You bet it is.

JOHN: Your language.

BUZZ: So sue me. That's from *Guys and Dolls*, for you kiddies.

RAMON: Happy Memorial Day.

PERRY: I think the point is, we're all sitting around here talking about something, pretending to care.

ARTHUR: No one's pretending.

PERRY: Pretending to care, when the truth is there's nothing we can do about it. It would hurt too much to really care. You wouldn't have a stomachache, you'd be dead from the dry heaves from throwing your guts up for the rest of your life. That kid is a picture in a newspaper who makes us feel bad for having it so good. But feed him, brush him off, and in ten years he's just another nigger to scare the shit out of us. Apologies tendered, but that's how I see it.

ARTHUR: Apologies not accepted.

GREGORY: Don't, you two.

ARTHUR: I hate it when he talks like that.

PERRY: You'd rather I dissembled, sirrah? (I wasn't an English major at Williams for nothing!)

ARTHUR: Yes. I'd rather you would. Rather the man I shared my life with and loved with all my heart, rather he dissembled than let me see the hate and bile there.

PERRY: The hate and bile aren't for you, love.

ARTHUR: That's not good enough, Perry. After a while, the hate and bile are for everyone. It all comes around.

(*He starts clearing the table.*)

PERRY: Anyway.

ARTHUR: I hate that word. You use it to get yourself out of every tight corner you've ever found yourself in. Shall I load the washer?

GREGORY: Just rinse and stack. Thank you, Arthur.

RAMON: Do you need a hand?

ARTHUR: No, thank you.

(*He goes.*)

PERRY: The younger generation hasn't put in their two cents, I notice.

RAMON: As a person of color, I think you're full of shit. As a gay man, I think—

JOHN: No one cares what you think as a gay man, duck. That wasn't the question. What do you think as a member of the human race?

RAMON: As a gay man, I think you're full of shit.

(*We hear a door slam.* ARTHUR *isn't coming back. Everyone reacts.*)

I think the problem begins right here, the way we relate to one another as gay men.

JOHN: This is tired, Ramon. Very, very tired.

RAMON: I don't think it is. We don't love one another because we don't love ourselves.

JOHN: Clichés! Clichés!

RAMON: Where is the love at this table? I want to see the love at this table.

BOBBY: I love Gregory.

GREGORY: I love Bobby.

PERRY: I love Arthur. I love Gregory. I love Bobby. I love Buzz. Right now I love you, your righteous anger.

BUZZ: I sure as hell don't love anyone at this table right now. All right, Bobby and Greg. A little bit, but only because they're our hosts.

JOHN: I love the Queen; she's been through hell lately. My Aunt Olivia in Brighton in a pensioners' villa—old-age home, you call them? My Welsh Corgi, Dylan, even though he's been dead lo these eleven years (I'm surprised his name came up!). And my job.

GREGORY: Thank you.

RAMON: Everything you love is dead or old or inanimal. Don't you love anything that's alive and new?

JOHN: Of course I do, but I choose not to share them around a dinner table. And you mean "inanimate."

PERRY: That's honest.

JOHN: I thought that's what we were all being. Otherwise, what's the point? Are you satisfied, Ramon?

RAMON: None of you said yourself.

PERRY: Maybe it goes without saying.

JOHN: We were waiting for you, Ramon. How do you love yourself? Let us count the ways.

RAMON: I love myself. I love myself when I dance.

JOHN: That's one.

RAMON: I love myself when I'm dancing. When I feel the music right here. When I'm moving in time and space. Gregory knows what I'm talking about.

GREGORY: Yes, yes, I do.

RAMON: When I dance I become all the best things I can be.

JOHN: Ramon loves himself when he dances. That's still only one, Chiquita. One and counting.

RAMON: I love myself when I'm making love with a really hot man. I love myself when I'm eating really good food. I love myself when I'm swimming naked.

JOHN: That's four.

RAMON: The rest of the time I just feel okay.

PERRY: I'm jealous. We don't reach such an apotheosis at the law firm of Cohen, Mendelssohn and Leibowitz.

RAMON: But most of all I love myself when I'm dancing well and no one can touch me.

JOHN: Is this as a gay dancer, luv?

RAMON: Fuck you, John.

BUZZ: You tell him, sweetheart. That's right: Fuck you, John.

JOHN: Americans use that expression entirely too often.

BUZZ: Everybody!

ALL BUT JOHN: Fuck you, John!

JOHN: In England we think it nearly as often as you do, but we don't actually say it to someone's face. It would be too rude. Half the people who are being knighted at the Palace every year are thinking "Fuck you" as they're being tapped with that little sword, but they don't come right out and say it, the way an American would, which is why we don't knight Americans, the only reason—you're too uncouth.

ALL BUT JOHN: Fuck you.

JOHN: What do you mean when you tell another person "Fuck you"?

RAMON: Fuck you, John. And don't you ever call me Chiquita again.

BUZZ: This is good.

JOHN: I think you mean several things. Mixed signals, I believe they're called in therapeutic circles. "I hate you. Get out of my life." At least, "I hate you, get out of my life for the moment."

RAMON: Fuck you.

JOHN: "I love you, but you don't love me. I want to kill you, but I can't so I will hurt you instead. I want to make you feel small and insignificant, the way you've made me feel. I want to make you feel every terrible thing my entire life right up until this moment has made me feel." Ah, there's the link! I knew we'd find it. The common bond uniting this limey and the Yanks. The resolution of our fraternal theme.

RAMON: I said "Fuck you."

JOHN: But until we recognize and accept this mutual "Fuck you" in each of us, with every last fiber of my fading British being, every last ounce of my tobaccoed English breath, I say "Fuck you" right back. Fuck you, Ramon. Fuck you, Buzz. Fuck you, Perry. Fuck you, Gregory. Fuck you, Bobby. Fuck all of you. Well, I think I've said my piece.

(*He moves away from the others, who remain at table.*)

I feel like playing, Gregory. Did you have your mighty Bechstein tuned in honor of our royal visit?

GREGORY: The man. Um. Was just here.

JOHN: What would you like to hear?

PERRY: I don't think anyone much cares.

JOHN: I'll play very softly.

BUZZ: I don't suppose you know *Subways Are for Sleeping*?

JOHN: Would anyone say no to a little Chopin?

RAMON: I would.

JOHN: One of the nocturnes.

(*He goes into the next room.*)

RAMON: I'm still saying "Fuck you," John!

BUZZ: What brought that on?

PERRY: His brother?

BUZZ: That's no excuse. Play something gay. We want gay music written by a gay composer.

PERRY: There's no such thing as gay music, Buzz.

BUZZ: Well, maybe there should be. I'm sick of straight people. Tell the truth, aren't you? There's too goddamn many of them. I was in the bank yesterday. They were everywhere. Writing checks, making deposits. Two of them were applying for a mortgage. It was disgusting. They're taking over. No one wants to talk about it, but it's true.

(JOHN *starts playing the piano, off.*)

JOHN (*off*): This is for you, Buzz. It's by Tchaikovsky. Peter Ilitch. One of us. Can't you tell? All these dominant triads are so, so gay! Who did he think he was fooling, writing music like this?

(*Melancholy music fills the room. They listen.*)

BUZZ: I like this. It's not Jerry Herman, but it's got a beat.

(PERRY *gets up.*)

GREGORY: Where. Um . . . ?

PERRY: I'd better find Arthur.

(*He goes.*)

JOHN (*off*): This is depressing. How's this, Gregory?

(*He starts playing the* Dance of the Little Swans *from* Swan Lake.)

BUZZ: That's more like it.

GREGORY: That's the. Um. Music. *Swan Lake*. The benefit. The *Pas des Cygnes*. Thank you, John.

(GREGORY *stands up from the table. He begins to dance the* Pas des Cygnes *from* Swan Lake. *He is an entirely different person when he moves: free, spontaneous, as physically fluent as he is verbally inhibited.*)

BUZZ: What are you doing?

GREGORY: The *Pas de Cygnes.*

BUZZ: I don't do *Pas de Cygnes.* What is it?

GREGORY: The *Dance of the Swans.* Come on. I can't do it alone.
Ramon!

RAMON: No, thanks.

GREGORY: Come on, Buzz!

BUZZ: Why are you holding your arms like that?

(*Indeed, as* GREGORY *dances he holds his arms crossed in front
of him, each hand on its opposite side, ready to link hands with
another person and form a chain.*)

GREGORY: I'm waiting for you to take my hand.

JOHN (*off*): What are you doing in there?

GREGORY: We're dancing! Don't stop! Take my hand, Buzz.

(BUZZ *tentatively takes his hand and will try to follow* GREG-
ORY*'s steps.*)

BOBBY: What are they doing?

RAMON: Now they're both dancing.

BOBBY: How do they look?

BUZZ: Ridiculous. What do you think?

BOBBY: You see? I knew it would be funny.

(RAMON *and* BOBBY *begin to laugh.* GREGORY *and* BUZZ *continue to dance while* JOHN *plays the piano from another room.*)

GREGORY: That's it, Buzz, that's it.

BUZZ: My admiration for Chita Rivera has just become bound-
less!

RAMON: You should see this.

BOBBY: I can imagine.

JOHN: Can I stop?

THE OTHERS: NO!!

GREGORY: Now you've got it!

BUZZ: Eat your heart out, Donna McKechnie!

(*Their arms linked,* GREGORY *and* BUZZ *dance themselves out of the house and out onto the grounds.*)

BOBBY: What happened?

RAMON: They're gone. They danced themselves right out onto the lawn.

(PERRY *has joined* ARTHUR *down by the lake.*)

PERRY: Listen to them up there. We're missing all the fun.

ARTHUR: We better talk.

PERRY: Okay. I brought you a sweater.

ARTHUR: Thank you.

PERRY: And one of their blankets. I thought we could spread it and look at the sky. The stars are incredible. Thick as . . . whatever stars are thick as. "Molasses" doesn't sound right.

ARTHUR: Thieves? No. Diamonds! Thick as diamonds on a jeweler's black felt!

PERRY: I love you.

ARTHUR: I know. Me, too.

PERRY: I'm sorry we don't always understand each other. I hate it when we're not in sync. I hate what I said at the table.

ARTHUR: I hated it, too.

PERRY: I just get so frightened sometimes, so angry.

ARTHUR: It's all right, Perry, we all do.

PERRY: Don't give up on me.

ARTHUR: No. I thought you were coming down here with me. It's spectacular. I can see Orion's Belt and both Dippers.

PERRY: That's not the Dipper. That's the Dipper.

(*The piano music stops.* JOHN *comes back into the room where* BOBBY *and* RAMON *are.*)

JOHN: Where is everyone?

BOBBY: They were last sighted heading for the boathouse. Gregory was very pleased with himself.

JOHN: You see, I'm good for something. I'm not entirely bad!

BOBBY: No one is, John.

JOHN: Thank you. I can't tell you how good that makes me feel. I was a shit tonight and I'm not even drunk. I'm sorry, Ramon. Am I forgiven?

BOBBY: Ramon?

JOHN: "Am I forgiven?" I said.

RAMON: Yes.

JOHN: Thank you. Forgiveness is good. We all need it from time to time. It's this business with my brother.

(*He goes back into the adjoining room and begins to play a Beethoven sonata.*)

BOBBY: Are you still there?

RAMON: Yes.

BOBBY: What are you doing?

RAMON: **Nothing.**

JOHN (*off*): This one is for me.

ARTHUR: He plays beautifully, the son of a bitch. The devil's fingers.

PERRY: So many stars, so many stars! Say a prayer for Buzz.

BUZZ: Arthur and Perry lay on blankets and looked at the heavens and talked things out. Gregory danced on by a couple of times. John played a melancholy piano until the wee small hours of the morning. Bobby and Ramon sat quietly talking across the deserted dining table—empty glasses, soiled napkins between them. All in all, there was a lot of love in Gregory and Bobby's house that first night of the first holiday weekend of the summer. It didn't start raining till the next morning. It didn't stop until the drive back home on Monday night. It rained all weekend.

BOBBY: It was raining when Buzz started crying in the middle of a movie on AMC and couldn't stop.

RAMON: It was raining when Gregory sat alone in his studio for six hours listening to a piece of music and didn't move from his chair.

BUZZ: It was raining when Ramon waited for Bobby by the refrigerator and he dropped the bottle.

ARTHUR: It was raining when John wanted Ramon to fuck him the next afternoon anyway.

PERRY: Anyway! There's that word again. And he's wrong, this one. I don't say "anyway" when I'm cornered. I say it when I'm overcome.
    I love you, Arthur Pape.

(*He kisses* ARTHUR *on the lips.*)

(GREGORY *and* BUZZ *will dance by again. They are having a wonderful time.*)

(BOBBY *and* RAMON *remain at the dining table.*)

(JOHN *is playing a Chopin nocturne.*)

(*The lights fade. The music swells.*)

Lakeside. Blaze of noon.

The MEN *are singing "In the Good Old Summertime."*

As they move apart, they reveal RAMON *sprawled naked on an old-fashioned wooden float at a distance offshore.*

One by one, they stop singing, turn around, and take a long look back at RAMON *splayed on the raft.*

Even BOBBY.

Finally, only JOHN *and* RAMON *remain.*

JOHN: **Anyway.**

(*He turns away from* RAMON *and takes out* GREGORY*'s journal and begins to read.*)

"Fourth of July weekend. Manderley. Promise of good weather. After Memorial Day we deserve it. John Jeckyll is arriving with his twin brother, James. Perry has already dubbed them James the Fair and John the Foul. John will also have Ramon Fornos, a superb young dancer, in tow. I thought they were over. Chances of finishing the first section of the new piece before they all descend on us looking slim. Bobby says he will stand sentry outside the studio

while I work. I tried to tell him our guests aren't the reason
I—Too late. They're here.''

(*Lights up on* PERRY, ARTHUR, GREGORY, *and* BUZZ *making
ready to play tennis doubles.* ARTHUR *and* GREGORY *are partners. So are* BUZZ *and* PERRY.)

(JOHN *is free to walk among them as he reads.*)

BUZZ: Which end of the racquet do I hold?

PERRY: That's it! Change partners. You show him, Gregory!

(*He crosses to* ARTHUR.)

BUZZ: Good teachers are patient.

(ARTHUR *is looking off to* RAMON.)

PERRY: What are you looking at out there?

ARTHUR: Nothing.

(GREGORY *has his arms around* BUZZ *in the classic "teacher's"
position.*)

GREGORY: Here, Buzz. Make a. Um. V with your thumb. Um.
   And forefinger.

BUZZ: Thank you. See how I respond to simple human kindness?

GREGORY: You bring your arm back like this, step into the ball,
   and pow!

(*They continue.*)

JOHN: "Buzz arrived alone again. We were hoping he'd bring
   someone. He looks thinner.''

PERRY: Try to keep your eye on this ball, not those.

JOHN: "Perry and Arthur asked if they could celebrate their anniversary with us. I warned them John would be here.''

ARTHUR: That wasn't called for.

JOHN: "Poor John. People don't like him."

(*He closes the journal and becomes "visible" to the others.*)

PERRY: I don't want to fight. I want to beat them in tennis.

JOHN: Who's winning?

BUZZ: We are. We're killing them.

JOHN: I can't believe it.

PERRY: You can't believe it?

BUZZ: Look who I have for a coach and partner. Why can't you have a twin brother?

ARTHUR: Don't make Gregory blush!

JOHN: What's wrong with mine?

BUZZ: He looks too much like you and acts too much like me. Where are all the men? There are no eligible men!

PERRY: Will you keep your voice down?

BUZZ: For what? We're in the middle of nowhere! Will I keep my voice down! You're a martyr, Arthur, a genuine martyr. I would have pushed him off your tasteful lower Fifth Avenue balcony ten years ago.

JOHN: Ramon is eligible, gentlemen.

BUZZ: I don't date dancers. I've made it a rule. It's very simple. Dancers don't want to date me. So fuck 'em.

JOHN: In Ramon's case, you don't know what you're missing. Does anyone want anything from the house?

GREGORY: There's tea in the. Um. Fridge.

JOHN: I'll send James down with it.

(*He goes.*)

PERRY: I've got another one: the Princes of Light and Darkness.

ARTHUR: Could we concentrate on winning this set?

BUZZ: So what's the score? A thousand to one? I'm really getting into this.

PERRY (*annoyed*): Love–forty! (*He cranks up for a serve.*)

BUZZ: Getting ready to serve now, the ever-lovely Dr. Renee Richards.

(PERRY *flubs.*)

GREGORY: Double fault. Game! Change sides.

PERRY: Fuck you, Buzz.

BUZZ: What did I do? Who won?

GREGORY: We did.

BUZZ: We did? We didn't do anything. I love tennis.

(*They change sides.*)

PERRY: You heard John: he's eligible!

ARTHUR: Perry.

PERRY: Lighten up. Your serve, Martina.

(*The game continues.*)

(JOHN *is heard playing the piano, off.*)

(RAMON *raises up and looks around. He shields his eyes with his hand, scans the horizon, and lies back down.*)

(BOBBY *appears. He is wearing a robe. He will advance to the stage apron.*)

BOBBY: When Gregory told me he thought John and Ramon were over and was surprised that John would be bringing him again, I didn't tell him that they were and that Ramon was coming with him because of me. I didn't tell him that when the phone rang Monday night, and then again Thursday, and there was no one there, and he kept saying "Hello? Hello? Who is this?" I didn't tell him it was Ramon on the other end.

(*He falls off the stage.*)

Don't anyone touch me. I don't want help.

(*He climbs back onto the stage.*)

And I didn't tell him what Ramon's mouth felt like against my own. I didn't tell him the last time we made love I thought of it. I didn't tell him Ramon whispered to me this morning. He would be waiting for me on the raft when I swam out there.

(*He drops his robe and goes out into the lake.*)

(JAMES *appears, wheeling a serving cart with iced tea and potato chips.*)

JAMES: It's not who you think. I'm the other one. When John stops playing the piano, you can start getting nervous again.

PERRY: Ball!

JAMES: My brother gave me the most extraordinary book. *Outing America: From A to Z.* I'm absolutely riveted.

PERRY: Ball, please!

JAMES: It gives the names of all the gay men and lesbians in this country in alphabetical order, from the pre-Revolutionary period (Pocahontas, I think her name was) right up to now, someone called Dan Rather.

PERRY: Ball, please!

ARTHUR: Which one of them is it?

BUZZ: It must be James. The grass isn't turning brown.

ARTHUR: I think he's attractive, Buzz.

BUZZ: Yeah?

PERRY: Goddamnit!

(PERRY *retrieves the tennis ball.*)

　　Thanks for nothing.

JAMES: I'm sorry?

PERRY: Just wait till you say, "Ball, please!"

JAMES: I haven't the vaguest notion what you're talking about, luv.

PERRY: Skip it.

(*He goes.*)

JAMES: I must say, and I hope you take this in the best possible way, for a young country, you've turned out an awful lot of poufters. In two and a half centuries you've done almost as well as we have in twenty. John Foster Dulles. Who is that? Is it a juicy one? Benjamin Franklin. Him we've heard of. Very into kites. Knute Rockne. Lady Bird Johnson. Americans have the most extraordinary names! Booker T. Washington. Babe Ruth. Buzz Hauser.

(*He settles himself to read as* PERRY *rejoins the others.*)

BUZZ: Whose serve is it?

PERRY: Still yours. Don't patronize us.

ARTHUR: We can always stop.

PERRY: No!

BUZZ (*to* GREGORY): What's the matter? Are you okay?

GREGORY: I'm fine.

(*He's not. He's tired.*)

BUZZ: Are you sure?

GREGORY: I'm fine!

BUZZ: What's wrong?

GREGORY: I don't. Um. See Bobby.

PERRY: Are we playing or what?

BUZZ: Time. Is that legal? Can I call time?

GREGORY: I saw him go into the lake. Um. He doesn't like me
   to. Um. Watch him swim. It's an honor. Um. System. And
   I'm not. Um. Very honorable.

BUZZ: Ramon's out there. He'll be fine.

PERRY: What is the problem, people?

GREGORY: There he is!

(BOBBY *appears at the side of the raft. He is winded from the
swim and just hangs there.*)

BOBBY: Hello? Anyone aboard?

(RAMON *doesn't move.*)

   Ramon?

(RAMON *still doesn't move.*)

RAMON: This time I would let him find me. I waited, not
   daring to breathe, while his hands searched for me on the
   raft. I prayed to our Holy Blessed Mother I wouldn't get a
   hard-on.

BOBBY: Ramon?

RAMON: My prayers weren't being answered. I thought I would
   explode.

BOBBY: Ow! (*He's gotten a splinter from the raft.*)

GREGORY: Ow! (*He's twisted something running for a ball and falls heavily to the ground.*)

BUZZ: Are you hurt?

GREGORY: No. Yes. Ow!

(BUZZ, PERRY, *and* ARTHUR *help him to his feet.*)

Get some ice.

BUZZ: What is it? Your ankle?

GREGORY: My ankle, my knee, everything.

BUZZ: Careful with him.

PERRY: Take his other arm.

ARTHUR: I've got you. Get him to the house.

(*They are helping him off.*)

GREGORY: No, the studio. I've got ice packs there.

(*They help him off in another direction.*)

(BUZZ *looks out across the lake to the raft.*)

BUZZ: Bobby!

(BOBBY *is still hanging on to the raft with one arm. He works on the splinter with his teeth.* RAMON *sits up and gently takes hold of* BOBBY*'s wrist.*)

BOBBY: Oh! Who's that?

(RAMON *takes* BOBBY*'s finger, puts it in his mouth, sucks out the splinter, and spits it out.*)

BUZZ: Bobby! Come in! It's Gregory! He's hurt!

BOBBY: They're calling me.

RAMON: I waited for you last night. I thought you'd come down. Meet me somewhere tonight.

BOBBY: I can't.

RAMON: I'll be in the garden after supper.

BOBBY: Not the garden. The boathouse.

(BOBBY *kisses* RAMON *this time, passionately, and then disappears back into the lake.* RAMON *watches him disappear. After a while, he will lie back down and sleep.*)

(BUZZ *joins* JAMES *in the shaded area.*)

JAMES: No! I won't even say it. It's not possible. Do you think? Dare we dream?

BUZZ: What?

JAMES: This book says John F. Kennedy, Jr., is gay.

BUZZ: That explains it. (*He has seen the rolling tray of refreshments.*) Is that for us? (*He goes to it.*)

JAMES: That explains what?

BUZZ: I've seen him in the Spike. It's a leather bar in Chelsea. He comes in with friends. Daryl Hannah, the Schlossbergs, Willy Smith.

JAMES: I don't believe it.

BUZZ: I'm the wrong person to ask. I think everyone is gay, and if they're not, they should be. (*He calls off to the raft:*) Ramon! Noon! Teatime!

(RAMON *doesn't react.*)

He doesn't hear me. He's going to burn to a crisp. Ramon! If that was my boyfriend, I would swim out there and drag him in by the hair.

JAMES: If he were my boyfriend, he could do anything he wanted.

BUZZ: I know what you mean. Maybe that's why I don't have a boyfriend. I'm too caring.

(*They are both looking out across the lake to* RAMON.)

JAMES: My brother has always had a good-looking man in his life.

BUZZ: Thank you.

JAMES: I beg your pardon?

BUZZ: He didn't tell you? It was when he first came to this country. Short and sweet. Six months, tops.

JAMES: I'm sorry. What happened?

BUZZ: We were both very young. I was too needy. He wasn't needy enough.

JAMES: I don't think John can love anyone.

BUZZ: Now you tell me!

JAMES: Perhaps one of us had better go out there and tell Ramon.

BUZZ: I'll let you break it to him. I don't think I'm his type.

JAMES: I don't think either of us is.

(*They are both still staring out across the lake to* RAMON *on the raft.*)

I enjoy looking, though.

(BUZZ *and* JAMES *sigh.*)

BUZZ: Is there a British equivalent for "machismo"?

JAMES: No. None at all. Maybe Glenda Jackson.

BUZZ: Do you have a boyfriend over there?

JAMES: Not anymore. What about you?

BUZZ (*shaking his head*): When the going gets tough, weak boy-friends get going. Or something like that.

JAMES: I can't honestly say I'm minding. Last acts are depressing and generally one long solo.

BUZZ: They don't have to be.

(BUZZ *finally looks at* JAMES.)

How sick are you?

JAMES: I think I'm in pretty good nick, but my reports read like something out of Nostradamus.

(*He looks at* BUZZ.)

I should have died six months ago.

BUZZ: Try eighteen. Do you have any lesions?

JAMES: Only one, and I've had it for nearly a year.

BUZZ: Where is it?

JAMES: In a very inconvenient spot.

BUZZ: They're all inconvenient. May I see it?

JAMES: It's—All right.

(*He pulls up his shirt and lets* BUZZ *see the lesion.*)

I have a lesbian friend in London who's the only other person who's ever asked to see it. I was quite astonished when she did. Touched, actually. Mortified, too, of course. But mainly touched. Somebody loves me, even if it's not the someone I've dreamed of. A little love from a woman who works in the box office at the Lyric Hammersmith is better than none. Are you through?

(BUZZ *kisses the lesion.*)

JAMES: Gwyneth didn't go that far. It doesn't disgust you?

BUZZ: It's going to be me.

JAMES: You don't know that.

BUZZ: Yes, I do.

JAMES: You learn to make friends with them. Hello, little lesion. Not people you like especially, but people you've made your peace with.

BUZZ: You're very nice, you know.

JAMES: Frankly, I don't see how I can afford not to be.

BUZZ: No, I mean it.

JAMES: So are you.

BUZZ: I didn't mean to interrupt your reading.

JAMES: It was getting too intense. They just outed George and Ira Gershwin.

BUZZ: Wait till they get to Comden and Green. Would you like me to bring you a real drink down? I know where they hide the good liquor.

JAMES: An ice-cold martini. Very dry. With a twist.

BUZZ: Is that going to be good for you?

JAMES: Of course not.

BUZZ: Does this make me an enabler?

JAMES: No, but it makes me your slave for life. I'll snitch a frock out of National Theatre storage for you. Something of Dame Edith Evans'.

BUZZ: What's the matter?

JAMES: I'm waiting for you to tell me she was gay.

BUZZ: She wasn't, actually. One of the two British actresses who isn't. I think Deborah Kerr is the other one. But all the rest—galloping lezzies!

(*He goes.* JAMES *looks after him and does not resume reading for quite some time.*)

(GREGORY*'s leg is being tended to by* ARTHUR. PERRY *watches squeamishly.* BOBBY *is with them.*)

ARTHUR: How's that?

GREGORY: Ow.

PERRY: Jesus, Gregory! I never really looked at your body before. I mean, except when you're on stage in a costume and lights and I'm in the fifth row.

GREGORY: Well, don't start now.

PERRY: It's amazing.

GREGORY: It's just old. Um. And very used.

PERRY: Your legs are like knots. And your feet. I can't even look at them. Doesn't everything hurt?

GREGORY: Yes. They have for years.

PERRY: Why do you do it?

GREGORY: I don't know. I just know I don't know what I'd do if I didn't.

ARTHUR: Why do you practice law?

PERRY: Law doesn't do that to me.

BOBBY: Gregory says a dancer's body is the scars of his dancing.

GREGORY: Bobby.

BOBBY: Isn't that what you say?

GREGORY: To you. Now it sounds pretentious.

ARTHUR: It's not pretentious, Greg.

BOBBY: The dances are gone, but his body's effort to do them isn't. Show them, Gregory.

GREGORY: Here's the Philip Glass.

ARTHUR: Look, Perry.

PERRY: I can't.

GREGORY: Here's the Bach-Schoenberg. Here's the Ravel. The Sam Barber. Here's the best one of all: the David Diamond.

(BUZZ *enters.*)

BUZZ: I can't leave you kids alone for a second! Bobby bwana, you be having a phone call in the Big House.

BOBBY: Thanks, Buzz. Show them *Webern Pieces.*

GREGORY: There are no. Um. *Webern Pieces* yet.

BOBBY: There will be.

PERRY: There better be. We've signed the contracts.

BUZZ: I can understand not having a phone down here, but what has he got against an intercom?

(BUZZ *and* BOBBY *go.*)

PERRY: While Arthur tended Gregory and I gaped at his life's wounds (his body didn't look old; it looked exhausted, spent—like that barren soil of Africa that can't produce anymore), and while James waited with more anticipation than he realized for Buzz to return, and while Ramon bronzed his already bronzen body even bronzer, Bobby was learning via a very iffy connection with a not very forthcoming sub-attaché at the American consulate in Jaipur that his sister, two years his senior, was dead. Valerie, I think her name was. Just like that.

BOBBY: What? I can't hear you. You'll have to speak up.

PERRY: It was a freak accident.

BOBBY: What?

PERRY: Something to do with a faultily installed ride at a fun fair at a religious festival celebrating the god Shiva.

BOBBY: How?

(GREGORY *will join* BOBBY *and put his arms around him from behind while he talks on the phone.*)

PERRY: A sort of swing you sat in that spun around a sort of maypole.

(ARTHUR *joins him.*)

ARTHUR: We never got the full story.

(*He rests his head on* PERRY*'s shoulder.*)

(JAMES *stops reading.* BUZZ *comes out of the kitchen, mixing bowl in hand.* RAMON *sits up on the raft.*)

BOBBY: Thank you for calling. (*He lets the phone drop.*)

GREGORY: Oh, honey, I'm so sorry.

PERRY: No one knew whether to stay or go. There is nothing quite like the vulnerability of weekend guests.

BOBBY: It's all so fucking fragile. So fucking arbitrary.

GREGORY: I know, I know.

ARTHUR: It's not what we want. It's what Bobby wants.

BOBBY: I want you to stay.

RAMON: We stayed.

BOBBY: Let's go upstairs.

(BOBBY *and* GREGORY *leave.*)

(*There is a silence. From the house* BOBBY *is heard howling his grief: a wild, uncontainable animal sound.*)

JAMES: Poor lamb. I'm afraid those martinis have made me quite, quite maudlin. I'm all teary.

(JOHN *is heard playing the piano, off: the* Pas des Cygnes *from* Swan Lake.)

PERRY: *Swan Lake.* My blood just ran cold. Gregory is serious about that goddamn benefit.

JAMES: So many costumes, so little time.

PERRY (*calling off*): Give it a rest, will you, John? (*He gives up.*)

JAMES: Gregory says you're a good sport and you'll do it in the end.

PERRY: Gregory is wrong.

ARTHUR: I'm working on him, James.

PERRY: And you're not getting up in any goddamn tutu and toe shoes either.

ARTHUR: My lord and master here. Do you want to go for a swim?

PERRY: I want to get some sun.

ARTHUR: We can swim and sun.

PERRY: You just want to visit your boyfriend on the raft.

ARTHUR: You want to talk about giving something a rest?

(JAMES *buries himself in his book and begins to read aloud.*)

JAMES: "No one who had ever seen Catherine Morland in her infancy would have supposed her born to be a heroine."

(BUZZ *has entered with more refreshments. He is wearing an apron, heels, and little else.*)

BUZZ: They said the same thing about me.

PERRY: Jesus Christ, Buzz.

BUZZ: What?

PERRY: You know goddamn well what.

BUZZ: No. What? This?

(*He flashes* PERRY.)

PERRY: Put some clothes on. Nobody wants to look at that.

BUZZ: That? You are calling my body "that"?

PERRY: You're not at a nudist colony. There are other people present.

BUZZ: I thought I was among friends.

PERRY: I'm sure James here is just as uncomfortable as we are, only he's just too polite to say so.

JAMES: James here is still reeling from the news about the Kennedy boy. You could all be starkers and I wouldn't bat an eyebrow.

PERRY: Tell him, Arthur.

ARTHUR: It's not bothering me.

BUZZ: Thank you, Arthur. I'm glad Isadora Duncan and Sally Kirkland did not live entirely in vain.

PERRY: Please, Buzz.

BUZZ: No. Close your eyes. Take a walk. Drop dead.

PERRY: What brought this on?

BUZZ: Nothing brought it on. Some people do things spontaneously. It's a beautiful day. The sun feels good. I may not be around next summer. Okay? This is what I look like,

Perry. Sorry it's not better. It's the best I can do. Love me, love my love handles.

ARTHUR: That's what I keep telling him!

PERRY: None of us may be around next summer.

(ARTHUR *starts undressing.*)

What do you think you're doing?

ARTHUR: Come on, I'll race you out to the raft.

PERRY: Go to hell.

ARTHUR: I can't believe you actually lived through the sixties, Perry. We only read about them in Kansas, and I'm less uptight than you.

PERRY: You know, I could walk around like that, too, if I wanted to.

BUZZ: Who's stopping you?

PERRY: I just don't want to.

BUZZ: I think she's got it. By George, she's got it!

(BUZZ *and* ARTHUR *do a little celebratory twirl before he braves the lake waters.*)

PERRY: I give up. I hope your dick gets a sunburn.

ARTHUR: Yadda, yadda, yadda.

BUZZ: That's the spirit. The world loves a good sport.

(ARTHUR *goes into the lake and starts to swim out to the float.*)

PERRY: Both your dicks!

BUZZ: I forgot my sunblock!

PERRY: Would you bring mine? It's on our dresser. The lip balm should be right with it.

BUZZ: I thought you were mad at me. I see! Get me waiting on you hand and foot and all is forgiven.

PERRY: Oh, and the Walkman. There's a Bob Dylan tape with it.

BUZZ: Bob Dylan? You sure you don't want Rosa Ponselle? Get a life, Perry. They've invented penicillin. You can actually pick up a phone and talk to someone in New Jersey now.

PERRY: I still like Bob Dylan—and don't tell me he's gay.

BUZZ: For his sake, I hope he's not. Would you date him?

PERRY: That's cruel.

BUZZ: I know. So's dating.

(*He goes.*)

(ARTHUR *has reached the raft. He is winded from the swim.*)

RAMON: I'll race you back in!

ARTHUR: What? No. I just got here.

RAMON: Aw, c'mon.

ARTHUR: No, I said. Give me a hand.

(RAMON *helps* ARTHUR *onto the raft.*)

RAMON: I'll let you catch your breath. Then we'll race.

ARTHUR: My breath is fine. We're not racing.

(*He flops on the raft.* RAMON *stays in a sitting up position.*)

RAMON: I hate the country. I fucking hate it. There's no cabs to get you fucking out of it. I like mass transportation. I like the fucking pavement under my feet. I like places that sell food that stay open all night. I fucking hate it.

PERRY: Should I be trusting my lover skinny-dipping with a horny Puerto Rican modern dancer?

JAMES: It depends on what makes you suspicious. Horny, Puerto Rican, modern, or dancer?

PERRY: All of them.

JAMES: How long have you two been together?

PERRY: Fourteen years. We're role models. It's very stressful.

JAMES: Two or three years was the most I ever managed. Mutual lack of attention span.

(BUZZ *returns.*)

BUZZ: Here's your desperate attempt to stay young, Mr. Sellars. *Blood on the Tracks.* Wasn't this originally released on 78s?

PERRY: Bob Dylan will go down in history as one of the great American songwriters. (*He puts on the headset and lies back.*)

BUZZ: He's no Lerner and Loewe! (*He is getting ready to settle down, too.*) Wake me if I doze off. I have a VCR alert for AMC. *Damn Yankees* at one-thirty. Gwen Verdon is hosting. Poor James, you don't have a clue what I'm talking about.

JAMES: I seldom know what any American is talking about. (*Reading:*) "No one who had ever seen Catherine Morland in her infancy would have supposed her born to be a heroine."

BUZZ: I love being read to. I feel five years old.

(PERRY *sings along with his Dylan tape.* JAMES *reads to* BUZZ. JOHN *is playing the piano.*)

(RAMON *smacks* ARTHUR *on his bare ass.*)

ARTHUR: Ow!

RAMON: You had a fly on you.
You know, you got a nice ass for someone your age.

ARTHUR: Thank you.

RAMON: You both do.

ARTHUR: Thank you.

RAMON: I really hate it.

(GREGORY *and* BOBBY *are in their room.*)

GREGORY: When is the body—?

BOBBY: Not until Tuesday.

GREGORY: So long?

BOBBY: Red tape. She always said there was nothing worse than Indian red tape. We're meeting it in Dallas. I'll fly down Monday.

GREGORY: I think we should both fly down tonight.

BOBBY: No. You stay here and work. I want you to finish the piece. It's more important.

GREGORY: It's all important. Why don't you want to go down there tonight?

BOBBY: We've got a houseful.

GREGORY: I'll manage.

BOBBY: We'll see.
Do you know what this music is?

GREGORY: No. But it's Russian. It's definitely Russian.
There are times I wish you could see me.

BOBBY: I see you, Gregory.

GREGORY: See me looking at you. The love there. I'm not—

BOBBY: I know.

GREGORY: It only happens when I'm alone with you. It's like a little present. I know this is a terrible thing to say right now, but I am so happy, Bobby. Thank you, God, for him.

BOBBY: You know how we tell each other everything, even when it's hard?

GREGORY: Yes.

BOBBY: I'd like to make this one of those times.

GREGORY: All right.

BOBBY: Memorial Day weekend.

GREGORY: Yes.

BOBBY: Something happened.

GREGORY: Why do I have a feeling I don't want to hear this?

BOBBY: Ramon and I.

GREGORY: Don't, Bobby. Don't.

BOBBY: We made love. I didn't want it to happen, but it did.

GREGORY: Is there more?

BOBBY: No. I'm sorry.

GREGORY: So am I.

BOBBY: This was better than not telling you, Gregory.

(GREGORY *is starting to have difficulty speaking again.*)

GREGORY: It's Scriabin. Um. The music, it's. Um. It's definitely Scriabin.

BOBBY: Talk to me, Gregory.

GREGORY: Have you. Did you. Do you. Want to. Again?

BOBBY: No, I'm with you.

GREGORY: You're. Um. Very lucky you. Um. Can't. Um. See right now, Robert. Go to Texas tonight. I don't want you in our house.

BOBBY: Where are you going?

GREGORY: Down to the lake. Don't. Um. Come. Um. With me. Um. It's back. That was brief.

(*He goes. Bobby comes forward to us.*)

BOBBY: Do you believe in God?
     Don't worry, I'm not going to fall off this time!
     Do you? I think we all believe in God in our way. Or want to. Or need to. Only so many of us are afraid to. Unconditional love is pretty terrifying. We don't think we deserve it. It's human nature to run. But He always finds us. He never gives up. I used to think that's what other people were for. Lovers, friends, family. I had it all wrong. Other people are as imperfect and as frightened as we are. We love, but not unconditionally. Only God is unconditional love, and we don't even have to love Him back. He's very big about it. I have a lot of reservations about God. What intelligent, caring person doesn't lately? But the way I see it, He doesn't have any reservations about me. It's very one-sided. It's unconditional. Besides, He's God. I'm not.

(*He goes.* ARTHUR *stirs on the raft.*)

ARTHUR: Sun like this makes you want to never move again. I feel nailed to this raft. Crucified on it.

RAMON: Sun like this makes me horny.

ARTHUR: Well . . .

RAMON: I bet I can hold my breath underwater longer than you.

ARTHUR: I bet you can, too.

RAMON: Come on, you want to see?

ARTHUR: No! If you're so bored . . .

RAMON: Come on!

ARTHUR: I don't want to. Play with someone else.

RAMON: Come on! *Venga*, baby, *venga*!

ARTHUR: I'm resting. It's a national holiday.

RAMON: Come on! You know you want to! Don't be an old fart! Who knows? We get down there together, who knows what might happen? Yeah?

(*He jumps off the raft and goes under the water.*)

ARTHUR: Damn it. You got me all—Shit. I was nice and dry. I'm not going in there. I don't care how long you stay under. You can drown, Ramon. I hope you can hear me down there. You're not getting me in. All right, Ramon. That's enough. Come on. Stop.

(GREGORY *appears at the side of the raft. He hangs there.*)

PERRY: I remember when Gregory bought this place. I was dead against it. "It's in the middle of nowhere. What are you going to do for fun?" Now it seems like bliss. No one for miles and miles. We could be the last eight people on earth.

BUZZ: That's a frightening thought.

JAMES: Not if you're with the right eight people. Who's that out there on the raft?

BUZZ: It looks like Gregory.

PERRY: Where's Arthur? He was out there.

BUZZ: You're looking good, Gregory!

PERRY: Arthur? Arthur? He was with Ramon.

BUZZ: We'd better put a stop to that. Arthur! Your mother wants you. Arthur! The MacNeil/Lehrer report is on. Arthur! (*To* PERRY *and* JAMES:) Help me. One, two, three.

BUZZ, PERRY, JAMES: Arthur!!

(BUZZ *starts coughing. He can't stop.*)

JAMES: Are you all right?

BUZZ: Ooooo!

JAMES: Here.

BUZZ: Thank you.

JAMES: Just get your breath. Lean on me. There you go.

BUZZ: Look at Gregory out there. He's lucky. He is so lucky.

JAMES: So are we.

BUZZ: Not like that. Not like that.

(*In the silence, we will begin to notice the throbbing, humming sounds of summer's high noon. The figure of* GREGORY *on the raft glows, shimmers, irradiates in the bright light.*)

(*Nothing moves.*)

JAMES: Listen. What's that sound?

PERRY: Nature.

JAMES: It's fearful.

PERRY: It's life.

BUZZ: It's so loud.

PERRY: Because we're listening to it. Ssshh.

BUZZ: I never—

JAMES: Ssshh.

PERRY: Arthur and I were in Alaska once. We flew out to a
glacier. When the pilot cut the engine, it was so quiet you
could hear the universe throbbing. I didn't know it did that.
It was thrilling.

(*Tableau. The three men do not move.* JAMES *has his arm around*
BUZZ.)

(GREGORY *is sitting on the raft with his knees pulled up to his
chin. He is crying. There is a distant but ominous roll of
thunder.*)

PERRY: Five minutes later, it was raining buckets. Thunder, light-
ning, wind. Everybody scattered.
James, take the hammock in.
Gregory! Come in! Lightning!

BUZZ: Auntie Em! Auntie Em!

PERRY: Buzz, run the flag down.
Where is my Arthur? Arthur!!

(ARTHUR *appears, fully dressed and dry. He will join* PERRY.)

ARTHUR: Your Arthur was gasping for breath on the other side
of the lake.

(RAMON *appears; he is not dressed and he is still wet. He is
laughing and playful.*)

RAMON: I knew I'd get you in!

ARTHUR: You scared me. I thought something had happened to
you.

RAMON: I wanted to stay down there forever. I wished I was a
fish.

ARTHUR: He was sitting on the bottom of the lake. When I swam up to him he pulled me towards him and kissed me on the mouth.

RAMON: I was goofing.

ARTHUR: Then he swam away.

PERRY: In all the excitement, the tragedy of Bobby's sister was quite forgotten. Where were you?

ARTHUR: Nowhere. I was swimming. Their door is still closed. You were right, Perry, we should have left.

PERRY: Don't do that.

ARTHUR: Do what?

PERRY: Disappear.

RAMON (*holding a magazine*): Okay, here he is, I found him. Gather round, gentlemen.

BUZZ: It was after lunch and Ramon was having a hard time convincing us of an adventure he claimed to have had on the island of Mykonos.

RAMON: That's him. I swear on my mother's life.

BUZZ: And I had sex with the ghost of Troy Donahue.

PERRY: First you said he was the model for Calvin Klein's Obsession. Now he's the model for—

RAMON: I can't keep all those names straight, but I don't forget a face and body like that.

BUZZ: You all know the picture.

ARTHUR: And you found this person in the same position sleeping adrift in a fishing boat?

RAMON: Yes. You ever been to Greece? There are a lot of fishing boats. Why won't you believe he was in one of them?

PERRY: And you made love to him?

RAMON: Not in the fishing boat. It started raining. We went ashore. We found sort of a cave.

JAMES: This is very Dido and Aeneas. I'm calling Barbara Cartland.

(*He goes.*)

RAMON: Why would I make up a story like that? It's too incredible.

PERRY: You're right, it is.

RAMON: Fuck you, all of you. I don't care. But the next time you see his picture or you're tossing in your beds thinking about him, just remember: somebody had him and it wasn't you. I know how that must burn your asses.

BUZZ: Go to your room!

(*He goes. The others stay with the magazine.*)

ARTHUR: Do you think he's telling the truth?

BUZZ: No, do you?

PERRY: The thought of Ramon and his possible encounter with the Obsession Man hung over the house like a shroud. We all wanted him and never would—

BUZZ: I bet he's got a rotten personality.

PERRY: Anyway.
        There is nothing like the steady drumming of a summer rain on wooden shingles to turn even this pedantic mind into a devil's workshop. I've got an idea.

(*He whispers to* ARTHUR *and* BUZZ, *who surround him.*)

(RAMON *and* JOHN *are seen in their room.*)

RAMON: I don't know people like you and your friends. I don't know what you're talking about half the time. Who the fuck are Dido and Aeneas? We used to beat up people like you where I grew up.

JOHN: Come here.

RAMON: Do you believe me?

JOHN: Do you want me to believe you?

RAMON: Maybe.

JOHN: So come here.

(RAMON *will take his time coming over to where* JOHN *is.*)

PERRY: Unfortunately, John and Ramon were not alone. Buzz and I had hidden in their closet. Our plan was to leap out at the moment of maximum inopportunity and embarrassment and then regale the rest of the household with what we'd seen and heard.

BUZZ: It'll serve John right.

PERRY: What does that mean?

BUZZ: Never mind. Squeeze!

RAMON: What?

(JOHN *kisses* RAMON.)

PERRY: It was a terrible idea. Arthur would have no part of it.

ARTHUR: Happy anniversary to you, too, Perry!

(*He goes.*)

PERRY: Is today the—I'm sorry, Arthur. Oh, shit.

JOHN: What's the matter?

RAMON: I thought I heard something.

PERRY: That was our last chance. We should have taken it.

JOHN: Sit down.

RAMON: You want to? Now?

JOHN: Sit.

RAMON: I'm a little sunburned.

JOHN: Sit.

RAMON: Aren't you going to lock the door?

JOHN: It's locked. Sit.

(RAMON *sits in a straight-back chair.*)

Put your hands behind your back. Feet apart. Head down. Ready for interrogation. My beautiful bound prisoner. Look at me. You look so beautiful like that. I think I could come without even touching you.

BUZZ: Oh!

RAMON: I think I could, too. Let me go.

JOHN: No.

RAMON: Please. The rope. It's too tight. My wrists, the circulation.

JOHN: Go on, struggle.

RAMON: I can't get loose.

JOHN: Look at me. Don't take your eyes from mine. Who do you see?

RAMON: No one. You! Let me touch you.

JOHN: Not yet. Who do you see? Who do you wish I were?

RAMON: No, I won't tell you.

JOHN: Yes, you will. Who? Look at me. Look at me! Who? Who do you wish I were?

RAMON: Kiss me. Gag me with your mouth.

(JOHN *kisses him.*)

PERRY: We knew what they were doing. We didn't have to see.

BUZZ: I was singing "99 Bottles of Beer on the Wall" silently to myself. It's a very hard song to sing silently to yourself.

RAMON: Who do you see? Who do you want in this chair?

JOHN: I don't know.

RAMON: Yes, you do. Everybody does. Who do you see? Who do you want here like this? Tell me, it's okay, John.

JOHN: I can't.

RAMON: Who? Come on, baby, who?

JOHN: Don't make me.

RAMON: I can't make you do anything. I'm your fucking prisoner, man. You got me tied up here. Gagged. Mmmm. Mmmm.

JOHN: His name was Padraic. The Irish spelling.

RAMON: Fuck the spelling!

JOHN: Padraic Boyle. He was seventeen years old. I was nineteen.

RAMON: I hear you. Seventeen and nineteen!

JOHN: He will always be seventeen years old and I will always be nineteen. Neither of us grows old in this story.

RAMON: What did he look like, this hot fucking stud Irishman?

JOHN: He was a fierce-looking ginger Irishman with big powerful shoulders and arms with muscles with big veins in them. You could see them blue through the white skin of his biceps. Always in hip boots and a vest.

RAMON: A vest? He was wearing a fucking vest?

JOHN: I'm sorry—undershirts, you call them.

RAMON: That's more like it. Fucking Fruit of the Looms, fucking BVDs, fucking Calvins.

JOHN: He worked for us. So did his father. We owned a fleet of coaches. Padraic and his father washed them. But that didn't matter. We were friends. He liked me. I know he liked me.

RAMON: Cut to the chase.

JOHN: Cut to what chase? There wasn't any chase.

RAMON: It's a movie expression. Get to the good part.

JOHN: It's all good part.

RAMON: Get to the sex. One night . . . !

JOHN: One day we started wrestling. It was summer. He was washing a coach (that's a bus), and—

RAMON: I know what a coach is. I've been to London.

JOHN: And Padraic squirted me with a hose and I got him with a bucket of water and then we started fooling around, and one thing led to another and we started wrestling, we were in the garage now, and suddenly Padraic put his hand down there and he could feel I was hard and he said, "What is this? What the bloody hell is this, mate?"

RAMON: What did you do?

JOHN: I put my hand on him down there and he was hard and I said, "And what the bloody hell is that, mate?" and we both laughed, but we didn't move.

PERRY: Even from the closet, we were beginning to share Ramon's impatience.

PERRY, BUZZ: Cut to the fucking chase!

JOHN: He stopped laughing. "Do you know what we're doing?"
I had no idea, so I nodded yes. He took off my belt and
wrapped it around my wrists. He raised my arms over my
head and hung them to a hook along the wall. I probably
could have freed myself. I didn't try. He took out a handkerchief and gagged me with it. Then, and this frightened
me, he ripped open my shirt. Then he unfastened my trousers and let them drop to my ankles. Then he undressed
himself and took a chair, very like this one, and sat in it,
maybe five feet away from me. He had some rope. He
wrapped it around his wrists like he was tied to the chair.
He'd gagged himself, too, with his own knickers. He looked
right at me. He didn't move. Not even the slightest undu-
lation of his hips, and then he came and all he'd let out was
this one, soft "oh." After a while, he opened his eyes,
asked me how I was doing and cleaned himself up. Then
he stood up and kissed me lightly on the lips. No man had
ever kissed me on the lips before. I wanted to kiss him back,
but I didn't dare. He moved to whisper something in my
ear. My heart stopped beating. He was going to tell me he
loved me! Instead, he said, "I've doused this place with
petrol. I'm lighting a match. You have three minutes to get
out alive. Good luck, 007." And then he laughed and
walked out whistling. He never wanted to play again. The
last time I saw him he was overweight, the father of four
and still washing our coaches. But that's who I still see
there. Every time. And that's why we hate the bloody Irish!

PERRY: Clearly the mood was broken. I felt a certain relief.

(GREGORY *appears outside their door.*)

GREGORY: Knock, knock!

JOHN: Yes?

GREGORY: Can I. Um. Get in there a sec?

JOHN: Sure.

RAMON (*playfully*): Maybe Greg can rescue me. (*He puts his arms behind him, struggles again.*) Mmmmm. Mmmmm. Help.

JOHN: Stop that.

(GREGORY *comes into the room.*)

GREGORY: Sorry. I need to. Um. Get a suitcase. Um. For Bobby.

RAMON (*playfully*): Mmmmmm! Mmmmmm!

JOHN: Ignore him.

(GREGORY *opens the closet and sees* PERRY *and* BUZZ.)

PERRY (*to* GREGORY): Ssshh. Please. I'll explain.

JOHN: Was it in there?

GREGORY: No. Wrong closet.

RAMON: Help! Mmmmm.

(GREGORY *goes.* BUZZ *manages to exit with him without being seen by* JOHN *or* RAMON.)

It sounds like Bobby's leaving. I want to say goodbye. Do you mind if we don't—

JOHN: Suit yourself.

RAMON: I'm not Padraic.

JOHN: And I'm not Bobby. C'est la vie.

RAMON: I don't know what you're talking about.

(*He goes.*)

JOHN: Wait up. I'll go with you.

PERRY: I suppose the next few moments could be called out of the closet and into the fire. John had forgotten his wallet.

People like John don't feel fully dressed unless they're carrying their wallets, even on Fourth of July weekends on forty-plus acres.

JOHN: You son of a bitch.

PERRY: I'm sorry.

JOHN: You miserable son of a bitch.

PERRY: It was a joke. It was supposed to be funny.

JOHN: You scum. You lump. You piece of shit. How dare you?

PERRY: I wasn't thinking. I'm sorry, John. I have never been sorrier about anything in my entire life.

JOHN: How fucking dare you?

PERRY: I will get down on my knees to you to ask your forgiveness.

JOHN: What did you hear?

PERRY: Nothing.

JOHN: What did you hear?

PERRY: I won't tell anyone. Not even Arthur. I swear on my mother's life, I won't.

(JOHN *spits in* PERRY'S *face.*)

JOHN: I hope you get what my brother has. I hope you die from it. When I read or hear that you have, then, then, Perry, will I forgive you.

(*He goes.*)

PERRY: I don't know which was worse. His words or his saliva. Right now I can't think of anything more annihilating than being spat upon. I could feel his hate running down my face. So much for the unsafe exchange of body fluids.

(ARTHUR *is trimming the hair in* PERRY'S *ears.*)

ARTHUR: I'm glad you're getting your sense of humor back. I'd like to flatten that limey motherfucker. I'm tired of "limey." Aren't there any other hateful words for those cocksucking, ass-licking, motherfucking, shit-eating descendants of Shakespeare, Shelley, and Keats?

PERRY: Come on, honey. Let's drop it.

ARTHUR: I don't go around hitting people or using words like "motherfucker," but that's how mad I am.

PERRY: Let it go. I love my bracelet. Thank you.

ARTHUR: Happy anniversary.

PERRY: I'm sorry I forgot. What do you want?

ARTHUR: Towels.

PERRY: Towels? That's not very romantic.

ARTHUR: The last time your mother stayed with us I could see she thought the towels were my responsibility. It's one thing for her son to be gay just so long as he's not the one who's doing the cooking. Towels and a Mixmaster!

PERRY: Who wound you up?

ARTHUR: That asshole did. Don't get me started again. He's just lucky I'm a big queen.

PERRY: Don't forget the left ear.

ARTHUR: And you're really lucky I'm a big queen.

PERRY: One thing you're not, Arthur, and never will be is a big queen.

ARTHUR: I know. I'm butch. One of the lucky ones. I can catch a ball. I genuinely like both my parents. I hate opera. I don't know why I bother being gay.

PERRY: I was so sure you weren't that first time I saw you. I came this close to not saying hello.

(PERRY *suddenly kisses one of* ARTHUR*'s hands.*)

ARTHUR: Where did that come from?

PERRY: Are we okay?

ARTHUR: We're fine. Don't rock de boat. It don't need no rocking. Fourteen years! Make you feel old?

PERRY: No, lucky.

ARTHUR: My first time in New York. You had your own apartment in "Green-wich Village." Exposed brick. I was so impressed.

PERRY: It's pronounced Greenwich. You're lucky you were so cute.

ARTHUR: The Mark Spitz poster right out where anyone could see it.

(BUZZ *crosses the room.*)

BUZZ: He's gay, you know.

ARTHUR: He is?

BUZZ: They're all gay. The entire Olympics.

PERRY: This is my roommate, Buzz. Buzz, this is—I'm sorry—

ARTHUR: Arthur.

PERRY: Oh come on, I didn't—

ARTHUR: You did.

PERRY: Why are we whispering?

BUZZ: I've got someone in my room. He's a Brit. I'm getting him tea.

(*Now* JOHN *crosses the room.*)

JOHN: Don't mind me, ducks. Just nipping through. Is that the loo?

(*He goes.*)

BUZZ: Don't say anything, Perry. I think he's cute. He's written a musical. I think I'm in love.

PERRY: Take it easy this time, will you?

BUZZ: Perry likes it rough, Arthur—really, really rough.

(*He goes.*)

ARTHUR: He was right—you did.

PERRY: Look who's talking!
    Do you want me to do your ears now?

ARTHUR: That was John? I'd completely forgotten. He and Buzz met the same night we did. We lasted, they didn't.

PERRY: I thought you were the most wonderful looking man I'd ever seen.

ARTHUR: Did you? Did you really think that?

PERRY: Unh-hunh.

ARTHUR: Ow!

PERRY: Sorry. When was the last time I did this?

ARTHUR: Don't make a face.

PERRY: I'm not making a face.

ARTHUR: I can hear it in your voice.

PERRY: I wouldn't do this for anyone but you.

ARTHUR: You know, if you really think about it, this is what it all comes down to.

PERRY: What? Trimming the hair in your boyfriend's ears? Oh God, I hope not.

(BUZZ *and* JAMES *appear. They are ready for a tutu fitting.* JAMES *motions* ARTHUR *and* PERRY *to come close.*)

ARTHUR: That and helping your best friends out by putting on a tutu for five minutes in front of three thousand people in Carnegie Hall.

(BUZZ *and* JAMES *have put a tape measure around* PERRY*'s waist.* BUZZ *drapes him in tulle.*)

PERRY: You're wasting your time, Buzz, I'm not going to do it.

(BUZZ *writes down the measurements.*)

BUZZ: She's a classic *Giselle* size, I should have guessed. Thirty-six! Whose measurements are these?

JAMES: Yours, luv.

ARTHUR: Is that good or bad?

JAMES: For a tutu it's a little big. For a gay man it's a disaster.

BUZZ: I'm not thirty-six! What metric system are you on? Let me see that. What are you laughing at? You're next.

(BUZZ *and* JAMES *pursue* ARTHUR *off.*)

PERRY: Anyway. The heavens cleared. The sunset was spectacular. The next day would be glorious. We would have a fabulous Fifth of July, sodden fireworks and strained relationships notwithstanding. Only the evening lay ahead.

(*The sound of crickets.* BOBBY *is waiting in the yard with his suitcase. It is night.* RAMON *appears.*)

RAMON: Hi.

BOBBY: Hi. Betty's Taxi is living up to their reputation. "We're on our way, Mr. Brahms." Five minutes, she promised, and that was twenty minutes ago.

RAMON: I have a sister, too. I love her very much. I'm sorry.

BOBBY: Thank you, Ramon.

RAMON: Where's your cowboy boots? They told me home for you was Texas. I thought you'd be in boots and a Stetson.

BOBBY: Home for me is right here. My folks are in Texas. Paris, Texas.

RAMON: Aw, c'mon. There's no such place.

BOBBY: French is my second language.

RAMON: You're kidding.

BOBBY: I'm kidding. The settlers had delusions of grandeur.

(RAMON *takes his hand.*)

   Don't.

RAMON: I'm sorry.

(*He lets go of* BOBBY*'s hand.*)

BOBBY: A part of me is, too. I can't.

RAMON: Does Gregory—?

BOBBY: No.

RAMON: That night by the refrigerator . . . ?

BOBBY: Any of it.

(GREGORY *appears outside the house.*)

GREGORY: You're still here?

BOBBY: They're on their way.

RAMON: Safe trip, amigo. I'm really sorry.

(*He goes back into the house.*)

GREGORY: I would have driven you. Um. In. Um.

BOBBY: We've got guests.

GREGORY: We both need time to think.

BOBBY: I don't. I'm sorry. I love you.

GREGORY (*he is angry*): Are any of you. Um. Gardeners? I'm especially. Um. Proud of what I've done here. Um. It's a. Um. Seasonal garden. Always something blooming. Um. Just as another dies. That's a. Um. Bobby knows the names of everything. *Dianthus barbatus.* That's the Latin name. Um. I can't think of the. Um. Common one.

BOBBY: Sweet William. It's Sweet William. And this one is rue. Bitter. Very bitter. Buzz says I would make a great Ophelia if I wouldn't fall off the stage.

GREGORY: He shouldn't. Um. Say things like that. Um. To you. (*He is crying.*)

BOBBY: And this is. Wait. Don't tell me.

GREGORY: It's a rose.

BOBBY: I know it's a rose. Connecticut Pride Morning Rose.

GREGORY: I'll never understand it. The will to know the names of things you'll never see.

BOBBY: It's one way of feeling closer to you.

(GREGORY *embraces* BOBBY, *but they don't kiss.*)

GREGORY: Hurry back to me.

(*He goes back into the house.* BOBBY *will stay in the yard until his cab comes.*)

(*The other men have gathered in the living room. The TV is on.*)

BUZZ: It's not my turn to clear up. I'm waiting for the musical remake of *Lost Horizon.* I never miss a chance to watch Liv Ullmann sing and dance.

JAMES: **May I join you?**

(*He sits next to* BUZZ.)

ARTHUR: **What's this?**

PERRY: **Open it.**

ARTHUR: **You didn't forget. You had me fooled.**

JAMES: **What are we watching?**

BUZZ: **The Dinah Shore Classic. Dykes playing golf in the desert.**

PERRY: **Do you like it?**

ARTHUR: **I love it. Look, guys. A solar-power calculator.**

PERRY: **For your work. Arthur's an accountant.**

RAMON: **Very nice.**

BUZZ: **Switching channels!**

(*We hear* BOBBY*'s cab tooting off.* BOBBY *takes up his suitcase and goes to it.* GREGORY *watches him through the window.*)

　　　Oh, look, the President's on MTV! He's made a video.

PERRY: **Only in America!**

BUZZ: **He's gay, you know.**

PERRY: **Dream on, Buzz.**

BUZZ: **Why not? We could have a gay president.**

PERRY: **It'll never happen.**

BUZZ: **We're going to have a gay president in this country, you'll see.**

PERRY: **It's the Fourth of July, Buzz, no gay rights stuff, please.**

(RAMON *gives the appointed ''signal.''*)

RAMON: Are we having dessert or what?

BUZZ: No dessert. You're too fat. We're all too fat.

RAMON: My friend in the fishing boat didn't think I was too fat.

BUZZ: Stay out of that kitchen. We're all on diets.

(BUZZ, JAMES, *and* RAMON *go into the kitchen.*)

ARTHUR: Go to CNN.

PERRY: Not a moment too soon. I'd like to know what's going on in the world.

(GREGORY *is apart from the others.*)

ARTHUR: Cheer up, Gregory. He's coming back.

GREGORY: Thanks, Arthur.

ARTHUR: That looks like Gore.

PERRY: It's a gay demonstration in Seattle. The Vice-President is out there speaking up for endangered species. I don't think we were included. Jesus! Did you see that? He whacked that guy with his nightstick right against his head. Motherfucker!

GREGORY: What's happening? (*He joins them in front of the TV set.*)

PERRY: Why do they have to hit them like that? Jesus!

(*They watch in silence. Appalling sounds of violence are coming from the television.*)

ARTHUR: I can't watch this.

GREGORY: Um. Um. Um.

ARTHUR: It's okay, Greg, it's okay. Turn that off, will you?

PERRY: What is wrong with this country?
   They hate us. They fucking hate us. They've always hated us. It never ends, the fucking hatred.

(*The lights in the room go off.* BUZZ, JAMES, *and* RAMON *bring in a cake with blazing candles.*)

BUZZ, JAMES, RAMON, GREGORY (*singing*):

> Happy anniversary to you,
> Happy anniversary to you,
> Happy anniversary, Arthur and Perry,
> Happy anniversary to you.

> Make a wish. Speech, speech.

PERRY: I'm married to the best man in the world, even if he doesn't put the toothpaste cap back on and squeezes the tube in the middle. I wish him long life, much love, and as much happiness as he's brought me.

ARTHUR: Ditto.

PERRY: Ditto? That's it? Ditto?

(*They begin a slow dance together.*)

JAMES: That's nice.

BUZZ: You don't have to go all Goody Two Shoes on us.

ARTHUR: Everybody dance. All lovers dance.

BUZZ: What about us single girls? (*To* JAMES:) You know you're dying to ask me.

(*He starts dancing with* JAMES. *There are two couples dancing now.*)

PERRY: So what was your wish?

(ARTHUR *whispers something in his ear.*)

> No fucking way, Jose. He still thinks you're going to get me into one of those fucking tutus.

(PERRY *now leads* ARTHUR. *They dance very well together.*)

(BUZZ *and* JAMES *are dancing closer and closer in a smaller and smaller space. Pretty soon they're just standing, holding on to each other, their arms around each other.*)

(GREGORY *sits apart.*)

(RAMON *watches them all.*)

Arthur, look.

ARTHUR: What?

PERRY: Answered prayers.

(*The two couples dance.* RAMON *and* GREGORY *sit staring at each other.*)

(*The lights fade swiftly. The music continues until the house lights are up.*)

Dawn. GREGORY *is alone in his studio.* PERRY *is sleeping with* ARTHUR. JAMES *and* BUZZ *are walking by the lake.* RAMON *and* BOBBY *are both awake.*

PERRY: Gregory was stuck. He had been since the beginning of summer. And here it was Labor Day weekend. You'd think he'd move on, but Gregory is stubborn. I don't know if I admire that.

(RAMON *steals from his bed.*)

RAMON: Bobby?

PERRY: So was Ramon.

RAMON: Bobby?

PERRY: I don't know if I admire that, either.

ARTHUR: You're taking all the covers.

RAMON: Bobby, it's me.

PERRY: You hear that? They are up to something.

ARTHUR: Mind your own business.

RAMON: He's out in the studio. I can see the lights. I won't do anything. I just want to . . . Fuck it. I'll be downstairs making coffee.

(*He goes.*)

PERRY: I wonder if Gregory had counted on Ramon showing up
with John. I remembered the time Arthur had been unfaithful and how badly I'd handled it. I don't know what to say
anymore and I certainly don't know what to do. "Don't
ask, don't tell." No, that's something else. I prayed for
good weather, took a Unisom, and wrapped myself around
my Arthur.

(*He rolls over and sleeps with* ARTHUR.)

ARTHUR: No funny stuff. Go back to sleep.

(GREGORY *puts on the Webern Opus 27 and plays the same
passage over and over.*)

BOBBY: Gregory's not stubborn. He's scared. He's started telling
people the new piece is nearly done when the truth is there's
nothing there. I want to tell him to just stay in the moment,
not to think in finished dances. That it doesn't have to be
about everything. Just to let it come from here. But when I
do he says, "What do you know about it? You're blind.
You betrayed me." It hasn't been easy since I got back
from Texas.

GREGORY: Shit.

BOBBY: I wish it were just the two of us this weekend.

(JOHN *appears with Gregory's journal.*)

JOHN: The lawns were brown now, the gardens wilted. The au-
tumnal chill in the air was telling us this would be our last
weekend. Soon it would be "back to school." Manderley
had changed once again, but I hadn't. Still hung up on Ramon and our rituals. Still reading what other eyes were
never meant to see.

(*Reading from the journal:*)

"James Jeckyll has decided to stay in this country. Buzz
says he will get much better care here. He will also get

Buzz. They are in love. I'm glad it happened here. Who could not love James? We have all taken him to our hearts. It will be a sad day when that light goes out.''

GREGORY: Shit, shit, shit, shit, shit!!!

(*He stops dancing in a rage of utter frustration. He picks up a chair and smashes it again and again until it is in pieces. He falls to his knees and begins to cry.*)

PERRY: I can't sleep. You didn't hear that?

ARTHUR: Will you leave them alone?

PERRY: Who?

ARTHUR: Other people. All of them. You're as bad as John. And stop taking all the covers.

PERRY: I'm not as bad as John. No one is as bad as John. I smell coffee. Do you smell coffee?

ARTHUR: That's it! I want a divorce.

PERRY: Are you awake now?

ARTHUR: Thanks to you.

PERRY: I'll bring you up some. How do you want it?

ARTHUR: Black with eleven sugars. How do I want it?

PERRY: You take it with milk, with Equal.

ARTHUR: Why is he torturing me?

(PERRY *rolls out of bed.*)

PERRY: It looks like rain.

(*He goes.*)

JAMES: I'm so cold, I'm so cold.

BUZZ: I'm right here.

JAMES: Two hours ago I was drenched in sweat.

BUZZ: Tonight'll be my turn.

JAMES: We're a fine pair.

BUZZ: We're loverly. I wouldn't have it any other way.

JAMES: I left England for this?

BUZZ: How are you feeling?

JAMES: Not sexy.

BUZZ: How are you feeling, really?

JAMES: "We defy augury."

BUZZ: What does that mean?

JAMES: I don't know. It's from a Shakespearean play we did at
the National. The actor who played it always tossed his head
and put his hand on his hip when he said it. I think he was
being brave in the face of adversity.

BUZZ: Would this have been Lady Derek Jacobi or Dame Ian
McKellen?

JAMES: I believe I have the floor! So, whenever I don't like
what's coming down, I toss my head, put my hand on my
hip, and say "We defy augury."

BUZZ: Shakespeare was gay, you know.

JAMES: You're going too far now.

BUZZ: Do you think a straight man would write a line like "We
defy augury"? Get real, James. My three-year-old gay niece
knows Shakespeare was gay. So was Anne Hathaway. So
was her cottage. So was Julius Caesar. So was Romeo and
Juliet. So was Hamlet. So was King Lear. Every character

Shakespeare wrote was gay. Except for Titus Andronicus. Titus was straight. Go figure.

JAMES: People are awake.

BUZZ: I'll get us some coffee.

(*He goes to the upstairs bathroom, where* PERRY *is standing with his back to us.*)

(RAMON *is making coffee and singing a Diana Ross song.* GREGORY *comes into the kitchen.*)

RAMON: Good morning, Gregory. The coffee's brewing. I woke up in my diva mode and there is no greater diva than Diana Ross. (*Sings a Diana Ross song.*) I figured you were working out there. I saw the lights. I didn't want to disturb you. How's it going? Don't ask, hunh?

(*He sings a Diana Ross song and undulates. He's terrific.*)

These are the exact movements that won me my high school talent contest. My big competition was a girl in glasses—Julia Cordoba—who played "Carnival in Venice" on the trumpet. Next to "You Can't Hurry Love" she didn't have a chance. But just in case anybody thought I was too good at Diana, I went into my tribute to Elvis, the title song from *Jailhouse Rock*.

(*He sings from the title song from* Jailhouse Rock *and dances. He's electric. He remembers the choreography from the movie perfectly.*)

I was turning the whole school on. Girls, boys, faculty. I loved it. If I ever get famous like you, Greg, and they ask me when I decided I wanted to be a dancer—no, a great dancer, like you were—I am going to answer, "I remember the exact moment when. It was on the stage of the Immaculate Conception Catholic High School in Ponce in the Commonwealth of Puerto Rico when—"

(*He slows down but keeps dancing.*)

What's the matter? What are you looking at? You're making me feel weird. Come on, don't. You know me, I'm goofing. ''Great dancer you *are*.'' I didn't mean it, okay?

(*He dances slower and slower, but he has too much machismo to completely stop.*)

Fuck you then. I'm sorry your work isn't going well. Bobby told me. But don't take it out on me. I'm just having fun. Sometimes I wonder why we bother, you know? Great art! I mean, who needs it? Who fucking needs it? We got Diana. We got Elvis.

(*He has practically danced himself into* GREGORY *and is about to dance away from him at his original full, exuberant tempo when* GREGORY *grabs his wrist.*)

Hey!

(GREGORY *leads him to the sink.*)

What are you doing? Let go.

(GREGORY *throws a switch. We hear the low rumble of the disposal.*)

What are you doing? I said. I don't like this.

(GREGORY *turns off the disposal. He grabs* RAMON*'s other arm and twists it behind his back. At the same time he lets go of his wrist.*)

Ow!

GREGORY: Put your. Um. Hand down the drain.

RAMON: Fuck you, no!

GREGORY: Do it.

RAMON: No, I said. Ow! Ow!

GREGORY: I said, do it!

RAMON: What for?

GREGORY: You know what for.

RAMON: I don't.

GREGORY: You know.

RAMON: Because of Bobby.

GREGORY: Because of Bobby? Did you say "Because of Bobby"? What, because of Bobby?

RAMON: Nothing. Nothing because of Bobby.

GREGORY (*slowly and deliberately*): Put your hand down the drain.

RAMON: No. Ow!

GREGORY: Do it or I'll break it fucking off.

RAMON: You're crazy. You're fucking crazy.

(PERRY *enters the kitchen area.* BUZZ *is right behind him.*)

PERRY: Jesus, Gregory. What are you—?

RAMON: He wants me to put my fucking hand down the drain.

GREGORY: Tell them why.

RAMON: I don't know.

GREGORY: Tell them why.

RAMON: He thinks me and Bobby . . .

GREGORY: That's why.

PERRY: Somebody's gonna get hurt fooling around like this.

BUZZ: Let him go, Greg.

RAMON: Ow!

GREGORY: I'll break it.

RAMON: All right, all right. I'll do it, I'll do it.

(RAMON *puts his hand down the drain.*)

Go ahead, turn it on, cut my fucking fingers off.

(GREGORY *lets go of* RAMON*'s arm.*)

GREGORY: Is that coffee. Um. Ready yet?

BUZZ: That wasn't funny, Greg.

PERRY: Are you all right?

RAMON: That wasn't about me and Bobby. That was about me and you.

GREGORY: Coffee, Perry?

PERRY: Thank you.

RAMON: You're old and you're scared and you don't know what to do about it.

GREGORY: Buzz?

BUZZ: Sure.

RAMON: I'm young and I'm not scared and I'm coming after you.

GREGORY: Ramon?

RAMON: That's what it was about. Yes, please, with milk.

GREGORY: One café con leche for Ramon.

RAMON: Thank you.

PERRY: Anyway. My stomach is up in my throat.

RAMON: I knew he wouldn't do it. I knew you wouldn't do it.

BUZZ: Macho man herself here.

RAMON: He's just lucky I didn't pop him one.

(GREGORY *turns on the disposal. Everyone jumps a little.*)

GREGORY: Sorry. Coffee grounds.

BUZZ: You're not supposed to put them down there.

GREGORY: Live dangerously. That's my. Um. Motto.

PERRY: Anyway. The incident was never mentioned again. Funny, the things we sit on, stuff down. The simplest exchanges take on an entirely different meaning.

GREGORY: Ramon. Would you. Um. Take this up to. Um. Bobby. Thank you.

PERRY: No, not funny. Amazing.

(GREGORY *returns to the studio, puts the music on, and goes back to work.*)

Anyway.
    We spent all day in bed. We napped, we cuddled. Arthur read the life of Donald Trump. Don't ask. We listened to the rain.

ARTHUR: It's stopped.

PERRY: Of course it's stopped. The day is shot. We'll all go out and get a good moonburn tonight.

ARTHUR: It's not shot. Come on, we're going canoeing.

PERRY: It's dusk. It's practically dark, Artie. No. Absolutely not. We went canoeing.

(*They begin to paddle.*)

ARTHUR: I don't believe the rain this summer. First Memorial Day, then the Fourth.

PERRY: It's simple. God doesn't want you to beat me in tennis anymore.

ARTHUR: That's not what it means. It means He doesn't want us to develop skin cancer from overzealous exposure to His sun in our overzealous pursuit of looking drop-dead good to one another. Look out for that log.

PERRY: That's big of Him. I see it.

ARTHUR: After AIDS, he figures we deserve a break.

PERRY: That's five dollars!

ARTHUR: I think we've stopped playing that game.

PERRY: Who won?

ARTHUR: Not Buzz and James.

PERRY: How did we manage?

ARTHUR: Depends on who you slept with.

PERRY: Fourteen years. I haven't been perfect. Just lucky.

ARTHUR: I've been perfect.

PERRY: Sure you have!

ARTHUR: Do you ever feel guilty?

PERRY: No, grateful. Why, do you?

ARTHUR: It used to be nearly all the time. No, first I was just scared. Then the guilt. Massive at first. Why not me? That lingers, more than the fear. We've never really talked about this. Paddle.

PERRY: I'm paddling.

ARTHUR: Every time I look at Buzz, even when he's driving me crazy, or now James, I have to think, I have to say to myself, "Sooner or later, that man, that human being, is not going to be standing there washing the dishes or tying his shoelace."

PERRY: None of us is. Are. Is. Are?

ARTHUR: I don't know. Are.
        You're right. It's no comfort, but you're right.

PERRY: Will be. None of us will be.

ARTHUR: Paddle, I said.

PERRY: Why not, not you?

ARTHUR: That's a good question. I wish I could answer it.

(JAMES *and* BUZZ *come into view in a canoe.* BUZZ *is doing the paddling.* JAMES *is up front.*)

PERRY: Can we just drift awhile? Look, there's Buzz and James. Hello!

ARTHUR: Can we finish something for a change?

JAMES: I feel guilty. You're doing all the paddling.

BUZZ: Good, I want you to. Look at the turtle!

JAMES: I'm going to miss all this.

BUZZ: Sshh. Don't say that. Sshh. Don't even think it.

JAMES: There's Perry and Arthur.

BUZZ: I don't want to talk to anyone. Just us.

ARTHUR: I think we're back to zero with this thing, but I'm willing to bend my shoulder and start all over again. What else am I going to do with my time? But the fellow next to me with his shoulder to the same wheel isn't so lucky. He gets sick, I don't. Why is that? I think we should both go together. Is that gay solidarity or a death wish?

PERRY: Don't talk like that.

ARTHUR: I will always feel guilty in some private part of me that I don't let anyone see but you, and not even you all of it; I will always feel like a bystander at the genocide of who we are.

PERRY: You're not a bystander.

ARTHUR: If you didn't save the human race you're a bystander.

PERRY: That's crazy. You sound like Buzz.

ARTHUR: That's how I feel.

PERRY: You're not a bystander.

JAMES: Buzz, could we go back now?

BUZZ: Sure, honey.

JAMES: Right away. I'm not feeling terribly well.

BUZZ: You're there.

ARTHUR: Hello! They see us.

BUZZ: We'll see you at dinner!

PERRY (*to* BUZZ *and* JAMES): You want to race?

ARTHUR: Perry!

BUZZ: What?

ARTHUR: Jesus.

PERRY: I'm sorry. I wasn't thinking.

BUZZ (*to* PERRY): What did you say?

PERRY: Nothing! It's all right!

ARTHUR: Let's go in.

(*They paddle.*)

PERRY: You're not a bystander.

BUZZ: Grace. I thought he said something about grace.

JAMES: I think I soiled myself.

BUZZ: We're almost there.

(*He paddles.*)

PERRY: Anyway. Anyway. That evening. I'm sorry. (*He can't continue.*)

JAMES: That evening it rained harder than ever. I'll do it. (I hate making someone cry.) There was talk of tar-and-feathering the weatherman.

PERRY: I'm sorry.

JAMES: A slight case of the runs, Perry. I'm fine now. My bum is as clean as a baby's. The best is yet to come. The real horror.

BUZZ: We don't know that.

JAMES: Yes, we do.

PERRY: I don't know what came over me.

ARTHUR: It's all right, come on, Perry.

(*They go.*)

JAMES: I thought I put it very politely. I mean, I could have said, "I shit myself."

BUZZ: We're all walking on eggshells. I'll draw your bath, luv.

JAMES: Was that "luv" or "love," luv?

BUZZ: For people who insist on spelling "valor" with a *u* and using words like "lorry" and "lift," you're lucky we have a lenient immigration.

(*He goes.*)

JAMES: Anyway. (If I'm going to fill in for Perry here, I might as well try to sound like him. Bloody unlikely!)

After my bath, Buzz (and I never remotely thought in my wildest imaginings that I would be making love to someone called Buzz and saying things like "I love you, Buzz," or "How do you take your tea, Buzz?"), this same, wonderful Buzz wrapped me in the biggest, toastiest bath sheet imaginable and tucked me safely into that lovely big chair by the window in the corner of our room. I fell asleep listening to my brother play Rachmaninoff downstairs. I would wake up to one of the most unsettling, yet strangely satisfying, conversations of my long/short life. And I will scarcely say a word.

(*He closes his eyes. The piano music stops. He stands up and looks down at the chair. He is* JOHN.)

JOHN: There's no point in pretending this isn't happening. You're dying, aren't you? There are so many things I've never said to you, things we've never spoken about. I don't want to wait until it's too late to say them. I've spent my life waiting for the appropriate moment to tell you the truth. I resent you. I resent everything about you. You had Mum and Dad's unconditional love and now you have the world's. How can I not envy that? I wish I could say it was because you're so much better looking than me. No, the real pain is that it's something so much harder to bear. You got the good soul. I got the bad one. Think about leaving me yours.

They have names for us, behind our back. I bet you didn't know that, did you? James the Good and John the Bad, the Princes of Charm and Ugly. Gregory keeps a journal. We're all in it. I don't come off very well in there, either. So what's your secret? The secret of unconditional love? I'm not going to let you die with it.

My brother smiled wanly and shook his head, suggesting he didn't know, dear spectators. And just then a tear started to fall from the corner of one eye. This tear told me my brother knew something of the pain I felt of never, ever, not once, being loved. Another tear. The other eye this time. And then I felt his hand on mine. Not only did I feel as if I were looking at myself, eyes half-open, deep in a winged-back chair, a blanket almost to my chin, in the twilight of a summer that had never come, and talking to myself, who else could this mirror image be but me?, both cheeks wet with tears now, but now I was touching myself. That hand taking mine was my own. I could trace the same sinews, follow the same veins. But no! It brought it to other lips and began to kiss it, his kisses mingling with his tears. He was forgiving me. My brother was forgiving me. But wait!—and I tried to pull my hand away. I hated you. He holds tighter. I. More kisses. I. New tears. I wished you were dead. He presses his head against my hand now and cries and cries and cries as I try to tell him every wrong I have done him, but he just shakes his head and bathes my hand with his tears and lips. There have never been so many kisses, not in all the world, as when I told my brother all the wrongs I had done him and he forgave me. Nor so many tears. Finally we stopped. We looked at each other in the silence. We could look at each other at last. We weren't the same person. I just wanted to be the one they loved, I told him.

(JOHN *sits in the chair.*)

JAMES: And now you will be.

(*Lights up on* GREGORY *dancing in the studio.* PERRY *returns to the stage.*)

PERRY: Gregory was working! The lights in his studio had been burning all that night and now well into the next day. Bobby shuttled food and refreshment from the main house while keeping the rest of us at bay. None of us had ever seen Gregory at work. He'd always kept the studio curtains closed. But this time it was as if he wanted us to watch.

ARTHUR: We shouldn't be doing this.

RAMON: Hey, c'mon, quit crowding me.

ARTHUR: I'm sorry.

RAMON: Watch Gregory.
   He is so good. He is so fucking good. I'd give my left nut to work with him.

PERRY: Ouch.

ARTHUR: Did you ever tell him that?

RAMON: I'm in a company.

ARTHUR: Not his. And I think the expression is "right arm," Ramon. He told Perry he thinks you're a magnificent dancer.

RAMON: He never told me.

ARTHUR: What are you two having? A withholding contest? Duck! He'll see us.

RAMON: I think he knows we're out here.

BOBBY: Someone's out there, Gregory.

ARTHUR: He's going to kill you.

(*He goes.* GREGORY *finishes the dance. He is exhausted.*)

PERRY: When Gregory finished, he knew he had made something good, something he was proud of.

GREGORY: It's done, Bobby. It's finished.

BOBBY: The whole thing? Beginning, middle, and end?

GREGORY: Yes! It's even got an epilogue. Give me a hug, for Christ's sake! No, give me a chair. You got an old boy-friend, honey.

PERRY: He also knew he would never be able to dance it. Not the way he wanted it to be danced.

BOBBY: What's the matter?

GREGORY: I can't do this anymore.

BOBBY: Your legs just cramped. Here, let me.

(*He massages* GREGORY*'s legs.*)

PERRY: It wasn't just his legs. It was everything. Gregory had begun to hurt too much nearly all the time now. He knew he'd never make it through a whole performance.

GREGORY: Ramon!

BOBBY: You let him watch?

GREGORY: I wanted him to watch. Ramon!

(RAMON *comes into the studio.*)

RAMON: I'm sorry, Gregory, I couldn't help myself. But Jesus, where does stuff like that come from? I would give my life to dance something like that solo one day.

PERRY: Ramon had obviously reconsidered his priorities.

BOBBY: What are you doing, Gregory?

PERRY: Gregory was suddenly a forty-three-year-old man whose body had begun to quit in places he'd never dreamed of, looking at a twenty-two-year-old dancer who had his whole career ahead of him.

GREGORY: You're good, Ramon. You're very good. You're better than I was at your age, but that's not good enough, you should be better.

RAMON: Don't you think I know that?

PERRY: What Gregory next said surprised everyone, but no one more than himself.

RAMON: You mean your solo? In rehearsal? So you can see how it looks?

GREGORY: It would be your solo at the premiere. New York. Early December.

RAMON: I don't know what to say.

PERRY: I can't believe people really say things like that. I mean, all your life you wait for the Great Opportunity and you suddenly don't know what to say. It reminds me of the time I—

RAMON: Where are you going to be?

GREGORY: Out front. Watching you.

RAMON: What about . . . ?

(*He motions toward* BOBBY.)

PERRY: Someone had to bring it up. It wasn't going to be any of us.

BOBBY: What about what?

GREGORY: Ask him.

BOBBY: What's happening? Don't do this to me.

RAMON: I'm asking you.

GREGORY: I'm fine, Ramon. Are you?

BOBBY: What's happening?

RAMON: When do we start?

GREGORY: The fifteenth. Ten a.m.

RAMON: I'll be there on the first.

GREGORY: You won't be paid.

RAMON: Is this a secret? I mean, can I tell people? I want to call my mother. Is that okay? She'll shit. She won't know what I'm talking about, but she'll shit.

(*His enthusiasm is spontaneous and infectious. He runs off yelling.*)

Eeeeeowww! *¡Dios mio!*

GREGORY: We always said I would stop when it's time.

BOBBY: Time. I hate that word, "time."

GREGORY: It's time, Bobby.

PERRY: You should have seen this man ten years ago, even five. No one could touch him. He's always been some sort of a god to me.

GREGORY: I just want to stay like this, my eyes closed, and feel you next to me, our hands touching. Two blind mice now. I didn't know I was going to do this, honey.

PERRY: Ever since I'd known Gregory, he'd been a dancer. I didn't think I would mind this moment so much.

BOBBY: You did the right thing.

(*They stay as* GREGORY *has described them.* JOHN *appears and stands very close to them.*)

JOHN: This is what Gregory wrote in his journal that day. "Bobby and I made love. We kissed so hard we each had hickeys afterwards. I don't think I'll tell him. When I feel his young body against my own, I feel lucky and happy and safe. I am loved.''

GREGORY: Okay.

BOBBY: You ready?

(BOBBY *and* GREGORY *get up and slowly leave the stage.* JOHN *stops reading, closes the book, and looks in the direction* BOBBY *and* GREGORY *have gone.*)

JOHN: ''And I am all alone.'' That's from a song. What song? Anyway.

(*He sits and stares straight ahead.*)

PERRY: Anyway.

(BUZZ *has returned.*)

How's James?

BUZZ: Don't ask. Like ice. I'm running his tub.

PERRY: Poor guy. How are you?

BUZZ: Weary and wonderful.

(GREGORY *appears.*)

GREGORY: Who's using all the hot water?

BUZZ: We are, Gregory, I'm sorry.

GREGORY: That's all right, that's all right. I'll shower later. Really, Buzz, it's fine.

(*He goes.*)

BUZZ: If this were a musical, that would be a great cue for ''Steam Heat.'' ''Really, Buzz, it's fine.'' ''I've got ding! ding! steam heat!'' Of course, if this were a musical, there would be plenty of hot water, and it would have a happy ending. Life and Gregory's plumbing should be more like a musical: Today's Deep Thought from Buzz Hauser.

PERRY: Musicals don't always have happy endings, either.

BUZZ: Yes, they do. That's why I like them, even the sad ones. The orchestra plays, the characters die, the audience cries, the curtain falls, the actors get up off the floor, the audience puts on their coats, and everybody goes home feeling better. That's a happy ending, Perry. Once, just once, I want to see a *West Side Story* where Tony really gets it, where they all die, the Sharks and the Jets, and Maria while we're at it, and Officer Krupke, what's he doing sneaking out of the theater?—get back here and die with everybody else, you son of a bitch! Or a *King and I* where Yul Brynner doesn't get up from that little Siamese bed for a curtain call. I want to see a *Sound of Music* where the entire von Trapp family dies in an authentic Alpine avalanche. A *Kiss Me Kate* where's she got a big cold sore on her mouth. A *Funny Thing Happened on the Way to the Forum* where the only thing that happens is nothing and it's not funny and they all go down waiting—waiting for what? Waiting for nothing, waiting for death, like everyone I know and care about is, including me. That's the musical I want to see, Perry, but they don't write musicals like that anymore. In the meantime, gangway, world, get off my runway!

PERRY: You're my oldest friend in the world and next to Arthur, my best.

BUZZ: It's not enough sometimes, Perry. You're not sick. You two are going to end up on Golden Pond in matching white wicker rockers. "The loons are coming, Arthur. They're shitting on our annuities."

PERRY: That's not fair. We can't help that.

BUZZ: I can't afford to be fair. Fair's a luxury. Fair is for healthy people with healthy lovers in nice apartments with lots of health insurance, which, of course, they don't need, but God forbid someone like me or James should have it.

PERRY: Are you through?

BUZZ: I'm scared I won't be there for James when he needs me and angry he won't be there for me when I need him.

PERRY (*comforting him*): I know, I know.

BUZZ: I said I wasn't going to do this again. I wasn't going to lose anyone else. I was going to stay healthy, work hard for the clinic, and finish cataloging my original cast albums. They're worth something to someone, some nut like me somewhere. That was all I thought I could handle. And now this.

PERRY: I know, I know. But it's wonderful what's happened. You know it's wonderful.

BUZZ: Who's gonna be there for me when it's my turn?

PERRY: We all will. Every one of us.

BUZZ: I wish I could believe that.

JAMES (*off*): Buzz, the tub!

BUZZ: Can you promise me you'll be holding my hand when I let go? That the last face I see will be yours?

PERRY: Yes.

BUZZ: I believe you.

PERRY: Mine and Arthur's.

BUZZ: Arthur's is negotiable. I can't tell you how this matters to me. I'm a very petty person.

PERRY: No, you're not.

BUZZ: I've always had better luck with roommates than lovers.

PERRY: I think this time you got lucky with both.

JAMES (*off*): Buzz, it's running over.

BUZZ: I adore him. What am I going to do?

(*The other men are assembling in the living room.*)

GREGORY: All right, everyone. This is your five-minute call. This
    is a dress.

(BUZZ, BOBBY, ARTHUR, RAMON, *and* GREGORY *will get ready
to rehearse the* Swan Lake Pas des Cygnes. *This time they will
put on tutus and toe shoes. They will help each other dress. Think
of a happy, giggly group of coeds.*)

(PERRY *watches from the side.*)

GREGORY: John? Are you ready in there?

JOHN (*off*): All set.

(*He starts playing.*)

GREGORY: Not yet! Not yet!

RAMON: Okay, let's do it!

GREGORY: Lord, but you. Um. Have big feet, Bobby.

BUZZ: You're heartless. Picking on the handicapped.

BOBBY: I'm not handicapped. Not anymore. I'm visually chal-
    lenged.

BUZZ: I'm sorry, doll.

BOBBY: That's all right, doll. It took me forever.

GREGORY: John, are you still ready?

JOHN (*off*): Yes, Gregory.

GREGORY: Tuck it in, Arthur.

ARTHUR: I beg your pardon.

PERRY: You see? That's what I keep telling him.

ARTHUR: If you're just going to sit on the sidelines and be a kibitz.

RAMON: Kibitz? What's a kibitz?

BUZZ: It's a place where very old gay Jewish couples go.

(GREGORY *claps his hands with a choreographer's authority.*)

GREGORY: All right, gentlemen. Line up. From the top.

BUZZ: We're in big trouble.

GREGORY: John? Are you ready?

JOHN (*off*): Yes, for the eighty-fifth time!

(GREGORY *claps his hands again.*)

GREGORY: Okay, everybody. This is a take. All set, John.

(JOHN *begins to play offstage and they begin to dance. They have improved considerably since they started rehearsing.*)

GREGORY: Very good. Very good.

RAMON: Ow! Buzz kicked me.

BUZZ: Tattletale. Shut up and dance.

ARTHUR: That's from *Gypsy.*

BUZZ: That's amazing from an accountant.

BOBBY: How are we looking?

PERRY: Actually, you look like you're having fun.

BOBBY: Well, come on then!

(JAMES *enters. He has put on his tutu.*)

JAMES: You started without me.

BUZZ: We thought you were resting.

JAMES: Don't stop. Let me in.

(*He links arms with* BOBBY *and joins in the dance. The others are apprehensive about his participation but try not to show it.*)

Left! I always want to go right on that step.

BUZZ: If you do and I hear about it . . . ! That was the punchline to a politically incorrect joke nobody dares tell anymore.

ARTHUR: But you will.

BUZZ: Absolutely.
Hervé Villechaize, the deceased midget, was talking to Faye Dunaway.

ALL: She's gay, you know.

BUZZ: Keep trying, guys. One of these days you'll get it.
Anyway. Hervé and Faye.

PERRY: Anyway. While my friends rehearsed and laughed and I watched and felt envious of their freedom (I couldn't believe that was my Arthur with them! My button-down, plodding Arthur!), something else was happening, too. Something awful. James collapsed.

(*Everyone stops as* JAMES *falters.* JOHN *keeps playing the piano, off.*)

JAMES: I'm fine. I said, I'm fine! Everybody, please. Back off. I just want to lie down a little.

BUZZ: I'll—

JAMES: No. I'm fine. Don't stop. Go on. You need all the re-hearsal you can get.

(*He goes.*)

GREGORY: John, will you stop. John, goddamnit!

(*The music continues.*)

RAMON: I'll tell him.

(*He goes.*)

ARTHUR: Buzz, maybe you should go with him.

BUZZ: Maybe you should mind your own business.

ARTHUR: I'm sorry.

(RAMON *returns.*)

RAMON: John's gone up to him.

BUZZ: Put on the record. That's how we're going to perform it
    anyway. The piano is for stop-and-start. We're beyond stop-
    and-start.

ARTHUR: We're one short again.

BUZZ: We'll live.

(*He starts taking charge, his way of being in denial about
James's condition.*)

   Let's go. Places, ladies. From the top.

RAMON: You're being replaced, Gregory.

BUZZ: Did anyone object to me calling them ladies? Speak now
    or forever hold your peace.

PERRY: I object.

BUZZ: You're not in this piece.

(*He claps his hands. This time we hear the Tchaikovsky in the
full orchestral arrangement. They begin the dance again.*)

(*The dance continues.*)

PERRY: I wanted to join them. I couldn't. I just couldn't. I was
    a dancer once. I was a good dancer. What happened?

GREGORY: Come on. Um. Perry. We need. Um. You. It's a. Um. *Pas de six.*

BUZZ: That sounds dirty. I wish it were.

(*As the dance proceeds, one by one the men will stop dancing, step forward, and speak to us.*)

PERRY: I have twenty-seven years, eight months, six days, three hours, thirty-one minutes, and eleven seconds left. I will be watching *Gone With the Wind* of all things again on television. Arthur will be in the other room fixing me hot cocoa and arguing with his brother on the phone. He won't even hear me go.

ARTHUR: You insisted on keeping the TV on so loud. Wouldn't buy a hearing supplement.

PERRY: I hate that word, "supplement." They're aids. Hearing aids. They're for old men.

ARTHUR: Three years later, it's my turn. On the bus. The M-9. Quietly. Very quietly. Just like my life. Without him, I won't much mind.

GREGORY: You're getting behind, Arthur, catch up!

BUZZ: I don't want to think about it. Soon. Sooner than I thought, even. Let's just say I died happy. They'd reissued *Happy Hunting* on CD and I'd met Gwen Verdon at a benefit. She was very nice and I don't think it was because she knew I was sick. Perry and Arthur said, "You know what Ethel Merman is going to do to you, telling everyone she was a big dyke?"

GREGORY: On the beat, Buzz, on the beat.

(JAMES *appears.*)

JAMES: I wasn't brave. I took pills. I went back home to Battersea and took pills. I'm sorry, Buzz.

(*He goes.*)

RAMON: I don't die. I'm fucking immortal. I live forever. Until I take a small plane to Pittsfield, Massachusetts. I was late for a concert. Nobody else from my company was on it. Just me and a pilot I didn't bother to look at twice.

BOBBY: I don't know.

GREGORY: You—

BOBBY: I don't want to—

GREGORY: You won't be with me.

BOBBY: I'm sorry.

GREGORY: What was his name?

BOBBY: Luke.

GREGORY: That's right, Luke.

BOBBY: You knew that. He knew that. He does that just to . . . What about you?

GREGORY: There was no one else. Not even close. You were the last.

BOBBY: I'm sorry, Gregory.

GREGORY: It was my age.

BOBBY: No.

GREGORY: It was my age.

BOBBY: Yes.

GREGORY: You—

BOBBY: I said I don't want to know.

GREGORY: Don't be afraid.

BOBBY: I'm not.

GREGORY: It will seem like forever.

BOBBY: I'm sorry I couldn't stay with you.

GREGORY: I. Um. Bury every one of you. Um. It got. Um. Awfully lonely out here.

(JOHN *appears.*)

JOHN: I didn't change. And I tried. At least I think I tried. I couldn't. I just couldn't. No one mourned me. Not one tear was shed.

(*Long pause. No one moves. Finally:*)

PERRY: Anyway.

(*The dance resumes and the Tchaikovsky is heard again. By this final reprise of the dance their precision and coordination is as good as it's going to get.*)

It was just about now when the lights went out.

(*The music stops and the lights go off abruptly.*)

Violent thunderstorms are taken for granted in this neck of the woods. So are power failures when you live as remotely as Gregory.

(*Already matches are being struck and candles lit.*)

The benefit rehearsal would have to wait.

BUZZ: There will be no performance of *Ze Red Shoes* tonight.

(*More and more candles are being lit.*)

When do you expect the power back?

BOBBY: Are the lights still out? Aaaww! It could be forever.

BUZZ: You don't have to sound so cheerful.

(*The stage is ablaze with lit candles by now.*)

ARTHUR: You know what's going to happen, don't you? We'll all be sound asleep and the lights will come back on and the music will start playing and we'll all be scared to death. Why is it that when the lights go off the telephones usually still work? Hunh?

BUZZ: Gay people aren't expected to answer questions like that.

PERRY: Speak for yourself.

BUZZ: I was. I usually do.
Whose turn is it to do the dishes?

BOBBY: I'll start.

PERRY: You cooked.

ARTHUR: Hey, no fair.

BOBBY: Who said life was fair? It certainly wasn't a blind person.

(JOHN *enters.*)

BUZZ: How is he?

JOHN: He's sleeping but he's better. He's a little better. You've all been so . . . There aren't words enough. Can I give anyone a hand? I want you to like me.

(JOHN *exits.*)

ARTHUR: Look out there. It's clearing up. There's a full moon.

PERRY: This is why people have places in the country.

BUZZ: Even gay people, Perry.

ARTHUR: Drop it, you two.

RAMON: You could practically read by that moonlight. The dishes can wait. Come on, Bobby.

BOBBY: It's wasted on me. Go on down to the lake. All of you. Make them, Greg. I'll join you.

BUZZ: He's a saint. He's gorgeous and he's a saint.

GREGORY: John? We're all going down to the lake.

PERRY: What's the weather supposed to be tomorrow?

ARTHUR: More rain.

(PERRY, RAMON, ARTHUR, BUZZ, *and* GREGORY *move to the rear of the stage, where they sit with their backs to us looking at the moonlight on the lake.*)

(ARTHUR *begins to sing "Harvest Moon." The others will join in.*)

(BOBBY *is clearing up.* JAMES *enters. He is wearing a robe. He watches* BOBBY.)

BOBBY: Who's there? Somebody's there.

JAMES: It's me. Forgive me for staring. You looked very handsome in the moonlight. Very handsome and very graceful. You took my breath away. I'm going to remember you like that. It's James.

BOBBY: I know. Are you supposed to be down here?

JAMES: No. And neither are you. There's a full moon and everyone's down by the lake. I saw them from my window. Come on. I'll go with you.

(*He takes* BOBBY *by the arm.*)

I have a confession to make. I've never been skinny-dipping in the moonlight with a blind American. You only live once.

BOBBY: If you're lucky. Some people don't live at all. I thought you were scared of that snapping turtle.

JAMES: I'm terrified of him. I'm counting on you.

BOBBY: Let's go then.

JAMES: I have another confession to make. I'm English. I've never been skinny-dipping in the moonlight with anyone.

BOBBY: I knew that.

(*They leave.*)
 (*The front of the stage and main playing area are bare. Everyone is taking off his clothes to go swimming now. One by one we see the men at the rear of the stage undress and go into the lake. As they go into the water and swim out, the sound of their voices will fade away.*)

(*Silence. Empty stage.*)

(JOHN *enters. He looks back to the lake. He looks up at the sound of a plane overhead. He looks out to us.*)

JOHN: Anyway.

(*He looks straight ahead. He doesn't move. The lights fade.*)
 (*BLACKOUT.*)

A Perfect
Ganesh

THE PLAYERS

MARGARET CIVIL, Handsome, good bearing, not noisy
KATHARINE BRYNNE, Vivid-looking, forthright, an enthusiast
MAN, Someone else in each scene
GANESHA, A Hindu god. He has an elephant's head. His body
    is covered in gilt.

THE SETTING

The play takes place during two weeks in India—getting there
and coming home, too.

THE TIME

Now. Or very recently.

For Don Roos

A Perfect Ganesh was originally performed at the Manhattan Theatre Club in New York City. It opened June 4, 1993. It was directed by John Tillinger, with scenery designed by Ming Cho Lee; costumes by Santo Loquasto; lighting by Stephen Strawbridge; sound by Scott Lehrer; and movement direction by Carmen de Lavallade. The production stage manager was Pamela Singer; the stage manager was Craig Palanker.

THE CAST
(in order of appearance)

GANESHA	Dominic Cuskern
MAN	Fisher Stevens
MARGARET CIVIL	Frances Sternhagen
KATHARINE BRYNNE	Zoe Caldwell

A C T   O N E

Silence. The lights come up slowly on a stage which has been painted a blinding white. GANESHA *is there. He is eating fruit and vegetables his followers have left him as offerings. He looks at us.*

GANESHA: I am happy. Consider. I am a son of Shiva. My mother was Parvati. I am a god. My name is Ganesha. I am also called Vighneshwara, the queller of obstacles, but I prefer Ganesha. To this day, before any venture is undertaken, it is Ganesha who is invoked and whose blessings are sought. Once asked, always granted. I am a good god. Cheerful, giving, often smiling, seldom sad. I am everywhere.

(*Music.* GANESHA *begins to gently dance.*)

I am in your mind and in the thoughts you think, in your heart, whether full or broken, in your face and in the very air you breathe. Inhale, *c'est moi,* Ganesha. Exhale, *yo soy,* Ganesha. *Ich bin; io sono. Toujours,* Ganesha! I am in what you eat and what you evacuate. I am sunlight, moonlight, dawn and dusk. I am stool. I am in your kiss. I am in your cancer. I am in the smallest insect that crawls across your picnic blanket towards the potato salad. I am in your hand that squashes it. I am everywhere. I am happy. I am

Ganesha.
They're coming!

(*Music stops.* GANESHA *stops dancing.*)

I can see them. I can see everything. They're just outside the international departures terminal, struggling out of Alan's sensible, metallic-blue Volvo station wagon. Not a skycap in sight. George is at home in Stamford watching a desultory quarter-finals match in the Virginia Slims Tournament coming live from Tampa on the Sports Channel. George doesn't particularly like women's tennis, but he is paralyzed this evening. He didn't even get up when his wife left. Katharine kissed the top of his head while he let his head roll to his right shoulder so that it connected with, lay against, her right hand resting there. But their eyes didn't meet. "Well, I'm off." He'll miss her, he knows that already, but he doesn't know how much. "You sure you have enough money?" He is always asking her that.

(*Lights up on* MAN. *He is* GEORGE.)

MAN: You sure you have enough money?

GANESHA: Alan and Margaret tooted once from the driveway.

(*An automobile horn sounds off.*)

"More than enough. Don't forget to water the ficus." She decided not to say anything about the children. "I'll miss you."

MAN: I'll miss you, too.

GANESHA: Two toots this time.

(*The automobile horn sounds again, twice this time: short, staccato toots.*)

The Civils aren't the sort of people you like to keep waiting. "I love you. Bye." And she was gone.

(*Lights down on* MAN.)

She was on her way to India. He would never see her again.

(*Lights up on* MAN. *He is an* AIRLINES TICKET AGENT *now.*)

MAN: Air India announces the departure of Flight 87, direct service to Bombay, with an intermediate stop in London. Now boarding, Gate 10.

GANESHA: You have to imagine the terminal more bustling.

(*He lightly claps his hands twice. At once, we hear the hubbub of excited travelers' voices.*)

Every seat is taken this evening. A Boeing 747 filled to capacity. It has been for months. It's the feast of Hali where I come from. (Even gods who are everywhere have to come from somewhere!) Entire families are going home for it. Men, women, children. Lots and lots of children. This is Air India, after all!

(*He claps his hands again: we at once hear children crying, yelling, laughing, playing.*)

Listen to them! How could I not be? Happy, that is. Is there a more joyful sound than children? A more lovely sight than their precious smiles? A sweeter smell than their soiled diapers? *There's* a place to bury one's face and know bliss! But I digress. They're here.

(MARGARET *enters. She has two large pieces of matched luggage. The bags are on wheels and she has no trouble pulling them along behind her. She also has a small, matching flight bag and a sturdy, ample purse.*)

MARGARET: Good evening. We're on your flight to Bombay this evening. There's two of us. Business class. Maharani class, I think you call it. I believe we already have our boarding passes and seat assignments. (*She hands him the tickets.*) I think we have adjoining seats. Mrs. Brynne has a window seat and I'm on the aisle. 15A and 15B. At least that's what we asked for and the travel agent assured us we had. I can't sit anywhere but an aisle seat. I'm claustrophobic. Actually, I hate to fly. No offense. I'm a terrible flyer, but I do it. This is the twentieth century. Too bad there's not a nice boat to India—Oops! Ship, ship, ship; I always do that!— to India. That should be 15A and 15B in business class. Maharani class! That's really very sexist. Shame on you. Shame on Air India. Is there a problem?

MAN (*head never up from his computer keyboard*): There shouldn't be. What is the name of the party you're traveling with?

MARGARET: A Mrs. Brynne. Mrs. George Brynne. Katharine Brynne. B-R-Y-N-N-E. I left her at the passenger drop-off with my husband. One of her bags flew open. But she's definitely here. We both are.

MAN: Let me try something. (*He types furiously.*)

MARGARET: Is the flight very full?

MAN: Not a seat.

MARGARET: That's what I was dreading. And lots and lots of children, all screaming, and running up and down the aisles all night! When I was their age I was left at home. I wasn't whizzing about from continent to continent, I can tell you that! The twentieth century! Isn't it grand, though! From here to India in what? How long is this flight? Something like eighteen hours, yes?

MAN: It's closer to forty-eight hours, actually.

MARGARET: What? Forty-eight hours! They told me it was eighteen!

MAN: Just a little joke.

MARGARET: Well, it wasn't very funny.

MAN: Eighteen swift hours.

MARGARET: That's what I thought.

MAN: Unless, of course . . .

MARGARET: Unless, of course, what?

MAN: Unless, of course, nothing! I'm sorry. You looked like someone I could have a few laughs with. I'm sorry. I don't exactly have the most exciting job or life of anyone who ever lived. A few laughs on the way to the graveyard, I suppose that's asking too much in this, the Götterdämmerung of American civilization.

MARGARET: Is there a problem or not?

MAN: Let's hope not.

MARGARET: If you can't give us aisle seats, I'm not going.

MAN: Who made these arrangements?

MARGARET: Our travel agent. Wanderlust Holidays. They're in the Town and Country Mall in Greenwich. A Mrs. Cairn made the booking, Edith Cairn, like the terrier.

(KATHARINE *enters. She has two large, ill-matched suitcases and an alarming amount of carry-ons: flight bags, a portable computer, a camera and a VCR, and a portable music system.*)

KATHARINE: "O for a Muse of fire." If I said it once, I've said it a million times and I'll say it again: "O for a Muse of fire" to describe all this. Words fail me. The entire English language fails me. If I feel this way in the terminal can you imagine what I'm going to be like when we actually hit India? I'm sorry, but this is all too much for a white woman.

MARGARET: Will you keep your voice down?

KATHARINE: So what's up, doc? What's the story?

MARGARET: We're lost in the computer. Leave it to Edith Cairn. She's your friend. I never liked the woman. Look at me: I'm a wreck. I told this nice young man if I can't have an aisle seat, I'm not going.

KATHARINE: I'm sure we'll be fine, Maggie.

MAN: I've got you on standby, just in case!

KATHARINE: *Gracias. Muchas gracias.*

MAN: *De nada.* Let's try another routing.

(GANESHA *has come up behind the ladies and now waits patiently in line behind them. He is wearing a bowler hat and carries a briefcase and a London* Times.)

MARGARET: I knew this would happen. A wonderful start to a trip. Tally-ho and bon voyage.

KATHARINE (*to* GANESHA): We're going to India for two weeks. I told my husband, "Enjoy TNT, AMC and canned tuna fish. I'm out of here."

GANESHA (*presenting his boarding pass*): Excuse me, but am I in order here?

MAN (*after a quick glance*): Yes, you're fine. Go right aboard. Have a nice flight, Mr. Smith.

GANESHA: Thank you very much.

(GANESHA *departs.*)

MARGARET: This is ridiculous. We booked this flight months ago.

MAN: That was your first mistake. Excuse me.

(*He makes another public announcement.*)

Air India announces the departure of Flight 87, direct service to Bombay, with an intermediate stop in London. Now boarding, Gate 10.

MARGARET: Look at you: you're exhausted already. I told you not to take so much.

KATHARINE: I'm not exhausted.

MARGARET: None of that is going under my seat. I'm not going to sit all the way to Bombay with my knees up to my chin because you insisted on bringing all that crap with you. I'm sorry, it's not crap. But I'm not going to be your porter, Kitty. You read all the books: travel light. If they had one common theme, one simple message, it was "Travel light."

KATHARINE: Let's not fight, Margaret.

MARGARET: We're not fighting. Do you have your passport?

KATHARINE: It's right here.

MARGARET: He's going to want to see your passport. Get it out.

(KATHARINE *starts looking for her passport in one of her travel bags.*)

Can I give you one travel tip, Kitty? You should always be ready to show your passport. Keep it someplace where you can get to it quickly, without holding everyone up.

KATHARINE: I'm not holding anybody up, Maggie.

MARGARET: I didn't say you were. It was just a tip. (*To* MAN:) How are we doing?

MAN: Have you ever been to Zimbabwe? Just a little joke. We're fine.

MARGARET: That's not your passport, Katharine. That's your international driver's license. *That's* your passport.

KATHARINE: What do I do with it?

MARGARET: Hold on to it.

MAN: Would these reservations be under any other name?

MARGARET: Of course not.

KATHARINE: My maiden name is Mitchell, if that's any help.

MARGARET: Why would I· make our reservations under our maiden names, Kitty?

KATHARINE: Hers is Bennett.

MAN (*making another announcement*): This is your final call for Air India's direct service to Bombay via London's Heathrow Airport. Air India's Flight 87, final call. Final boarding, Gate 10. All aboard, please.

MARGARET: Now what exactly is going on here?

MAN: I'm afraid you two ladies have vanished without a trace into the vast netherworld of our computer system.

MARGARET: Is that supposed to be funny, too?

KATHARINE: It's not his fault, Margaret. He didn't do it on purpose.

MARGARET: I want those two seats.

MAN: I can't. They're being occupied by a Mr. and Mrs. D. M. Chandra of Hyderabad.

MARGARET: They're our seats. We booked them months ago. Mr. and Mrs. D. M. Whatever will just have to catch the next flight. Or put them in the back of the plane in tourist class.

MAN: We don't call it that. We call it leper class. All right, all right, Mrs. Civil! I'll tell you what I will do.

MARGARET: No, I will tell you what I will do if you don't give us those seats.

KATHARINE: Give him a chance, Margaret.

MARGARET: No one is sticking me back in tourist class with a lot of noisy children and natives. Some of them looked like peasants. Shepherds. I wouldn't be surprised if there were a few goats on board.

MAN: That's honest.

MARGARET: I want to see India my way, from a comfortable seat, somewhat at a distance.

KATHARINE: That's terrible, Margaret.

MARGARET: So, in the inimitable words of my traveling companion, Mrs. Brynne here, what's up, doc? What's the story, Air India?

MAN: I'm afraid business class is completely full. So is tourist.

MARGARET: This is outrageous. I'm going to call that travel agent.

MAN: All I have are two seats in first class, sleeperettes.

KATHARINE: We couldn't possibly afford that.

MAN: It's a complimentary upgrade, Mrs. Brynne. It's our error. Would that be satisfactory?

KATHARINE: Satisfactory? It's fabulous. Thank you. First class! What's your name?

MAN: Lennie. Leonard Tuck.

KATHARINE: I'm going to write them a letter telling them how wonderful you were to us. Tuck. Leonard Tuck. Like Friar Tuck.

MAN: *Gracias.*

KATHARINE: *De nada.*

MAN: Will first class be satisfactory, Mrs. Civil?

MARGARET: Of course it will. But I would have been perfectly happy in our own seats.

KATHARINE: What a beginning! What luck! First class! O for a Muse of you know what!

MAN: Abracadabra!

(*The computer whirs. Tickets and boarding passes emerge.*)

See how easy that was, Mrs. Civil? (*Making another announcement:*) Final call. Air India, Flight 87, direct service to Bombay. Final call, please.

MARGARET: Come on, Katharine.

(*She goes.*)

KATHARINE: Goodbye, America. Goodbye, husband and children. Goodbye, Greenwich, Connecticut. Goodbye, Air India terminal. Goodbye, Leonard Tuck.

MAN: Bon voyage, Mrs. Brynne.

(KATHARINE *goes. She leaves one of her flight bags behind.* MAN *closes down quickly and is gone.* GANESHA *reappears.*)

GANESHA: They're on their way. Well, almost!

(KATHARINE *rushes back on.*)

KATHARINE: My flight bag! I had a flight bag.

GANESHA: She doesn't see it.

KATHARINE: Did anyone see a flight bag?

GANESHA: Or me. I have that power.

KATHARINE: Hello?

(*She rushes off at the sound of the jets revving up. The sounds will grow.*)

GANESHA: It begins. Well, it all began long ago. World without end, amen, and all that. This particular adventure, I was meaning. These two little, insignificant, magnificent lives.

(*He is shouting to be heard over the roar of the jet engines.*)

> Can you hear me? Did you hear me? I said, these two little, insignificant, magnificent lives! I'll see you aboard at thirty-six thousand feet. Wait for me!

(*Sounds reach a deafening volume as* GANESHA *hurries aboard. The stage is bare except for Katharine's flight bag.* MAN *enters. He is a* THIEF. *He picks up the flight bag and rifles through it as he exits through the audience, scattering things he doesn't want in the aisles.*)

(*Sounds and lights reach maximum intensity, then quickly level off: the lights to the level of an airplane in the middle of the night; the sounds to the gentle, steady thrust of jet engines at cruising speed.*)

SCENE TWO

MARGARET *and* KATHARINE *are seated in the first-class cabin. They both have headsets on.* MARGARET *is watching the movie.* KATHARINE *is listening to a cassette.*

MOVIE SOUNDTRACK: I don't think you know what love is. Not real love. Love that enriches, love that lifts up, love that ennobles. I'm talking about love in its profoundest sense. Love as everything.

CASSETTE TAPE: All right, now that you've visualized your 10 Personal Power Goals, I want you to *choose* them. It's not I *want* to lose weight or I *want* to make a million dollars but I *choose* to meet the perfect mate, I *choose* to drive a Lexus Infinity. Ready? Take a deep breath. Hold it.

(KATHARINE *inhales.*)

MOVIE SOUNDTRACK: I think you understand obsession. I think you understand control. I think you understand passion. God knows, you know how to pleasure a person with your body. There's a word for people like you—the French have one, every language does—*fatal*.

CASSETTE TAPE: These are vocal affirmations. I want to hear you. Don't be shy. That's right, I'm talking to you! All right, go. I choose—!

KATHARINE: I choose to be happy.

MARGARET: After all that and they're still going to make love!

KATHARINE: I choose to be healthy.

MARGARET: The movies think that's the solution to everything! A lot they know!

KATHARINE: I choose to be good.

MARGARET: I'm very surprised at Air India for showing such a film. I wonder what an Indian thinks when they see—!

KATHARINE: I choose to be—!

(*The plane heaves.*)

MARGARET: What was that?

KATHARINE: What was what?

MARGARET: The plane, it jiggled.

KATHARINE: It didn't jiggle.

MARGARET: Well, it did something it shouldn't. There it goes again!

KATHARINE: It's just a little turbulence. I choose—Now I've forgotten what I choose. I choose to be happy. I already said that.

MARGARET: I hate this. I hate it, I hate it.

KATHARINE: Just think of it as a bumpy road.

MARGARET: What?

KATHARINE: It will be over soon.

MARGARET: How soon?

KATHARINE: I don't know. Soon. Soon, soon.

MARGARET: We should have gone TWA.

KATHARINE: TWA is for sissies. Anyone can go TWA. Air India is an adventure. I feel like we're already there.

(MAN *appears. He is a* STEWARD.)

MAN: Ladies! Sshh! Please. Your headsets, you're too loud. People are sleeping.

KATHARINE: Will you tell my friend we're not going to crash?

MAN: We're not going to crash. That's the good news. The bad news is we'll be starting dinner service just as soon as we're out of this. That was a joke.

MARGARET: I'm quite aware of that. Tell me, does everyone connected with Air India think they're a comedian?

MAN: People think Indians are humorless. They think we're funny, but they think we're humorless.

MARGARET: You're not funny and you're not an Indian.

MAN: On my mother's side. Her father was born in Calcutta. I was born on Teller Avenue in the Bronx. Whoa! Ride 'em, cowboy! That was a good one. It's always a little dicey over this part of the Atlantic this time of the year.

(*The plane heaves.*)

Ride 'em, cowboy! I better get back to my seat. The pilot has the Fasten Seat Belt sign on for the crew now, too. Excuse me. I shall return with your pickled herring and hot towels. The towels are tastier.

(*He goes.*)

KATHARINE: Does he remind you of Walter?

MARGARET: The steward? Not in the least.

KATHARINE: I didn't know you were afraid of flying.

MARGARET: I've flown over this part of the Atlantic this time of the year at least fifteen times and it was never like this.

KATHARINE: Actually, I like a little turbulence.

MARGARET: You're the type who would.

KATHARINE: It lets me know we're really up there. If it gets too quiet and still, I worry the engines have stopped and we're just going to plummet to the earth.

MARGARET: Can we talk about something else?

KATHARINE: Do you want to hold my hand?

MARGARET: Of course not.

KATHARINE: Do you want some gum?

MARGARET: Is it the kind that sticks to your crowns?

KATHARINE: I don't know.

MARGARET: If it's the kind that sticks I don't want it.

KATHARINE: You're out of luck. It must have been in the bag I left in the terminal.

MARGARET: What's that?

KATHARINE: A whistle. George made me take it. In case we get into any sort of trouble in India, I'm supposed to blow it so help will come. "Who?" I asked him. "Sabu on an elephant?"

MARGARET: Will you keep your voice down?

(The plane heaves, extra-mightily this time.)

KATHARINE: This is ridiculous. Give me your hand.

MARGARET: We're all going to die.

KATHARINE: Just shut up and say a Hail Mary.

MARGARET: Methodists don't say Hail Mary.

KATHARINE: We're going to be all right.

MARGARET: Ow! That's too tight!

(The turbulence subsides.)

KATHARINE: See?

MARGARET: I can bear anything as long as I know it's going to end.

KATHARINE: Remember the last year we went to St. Kitts?

MARGARET: The men got sick from eating crayfish.

KATHARINE: They were *langoustes*.

MARGARET: They looked like crayfish.

KATHARINE: That's not the reason I never wanted to go back there.

MARGARET: Alan nearly died. Besides, it was time for a new island.

KATHARINE: It was the incident with the little plane.

MARGARET: What incident? I don't remember.

KATHARINE: Yes, you do! We were swimming in front of the hotel. A small, single-engine plane had taken off from the airport. The engine kept stalling. No one moved. It was terrifying. That little plane just floating there. No sound. No sound at all. Like a kite without a string. I don't think I've ever felt so helpless.

MARGARET: I remember.

KATHARINE: Finally, I guess the pilot made the necessary adjustments, the engine caught and stayed caught, and the little plane flew away, as if nothing had happened, and we finished swimming and played tennis and after lunch you bought that Lalique vase I could still kick myself for letting you have.

MARGARET: You've envied me that piece of Lalique all these years? It's yours.

KATHARINE: I don't want it.

MARGARET: Really, I insist, Kitty. I think I only bought it because I knew you wanted it. That, and I was mad at Alan for some crack about how I looked in my new bathing suit. The plane's stopped jiggling. Smooth as glass now.

KATHARINE: I've thought about that little plane a lot. Maybe we were helpless. Maybe we weren't responsible. Maybe it wasn't our fault. But what kept that plane up there? God? A god? Some benevolence? Prayer? Our prayers? I think everyone on that beach was praying that morning in their particular way. So maybe we aren't so helpless. Maybe we are responsible. Maybe it is our fault what happens. Maybe, maybe, maybe.

MARGARET: Do you want to give me my hand back?

KATHARINE: I'm sorry. Thank you. Did I do that? I *was* holding tight! I'm sorry.

(*She kisses* MARGARET*'s hand.*)

What happened to your liver spots? You used to have great big liver spots.

MARGARET: Will you keep your voice down? I keep begging you to come with me. The man's a genius. And it's paradise there.

KATHARINE: And it costs three thousand dollars a week. I'd rather go to India for my soul than some spa in Orange County for the backs of my hands.

MARGARET: Happily, you can afford both.

KATHARINE: I keep thinking about Walter.

MARGARET: Why would you do that to yourself?

KATHARINE: I can't help it.

MARGARET: Well, stop. Stop right now. Think about something else. Think about the Taj Mahal. Think about India.

KATHARINE: They say it's like a dream, the Taj Mahal.

MARGARET: I hope it's not like the Eiffel Tower. All your life you look at pictures of the Eiffel Tower and then when you actually see it, it looks just like the pictures of it. There's no resonance when you look at the Eiffel Tower. I'm expecting some resonance from the Taj Mahal. I'll be terribly disappointed if there isn't any. You're humming again, Kitty.

KATHARINE: I'm sorry.

MARGARET: You asked me to tell you.

KATHARINE: All of a sudden, I can't remember when it was built!

MARGARET: It was begun in 1632 and completed in 1654.

KATHARINE: All that reading up on it and for what?!

MARGARET: Do you remember who it was built for?

KATHARINE: Of course I do. Someone's wife.

MARGARET: Everyone knows that, Kitty. What was her name?

KATHARINE: I knew you were going to ask me that. Marilyn? Betty? Betty Mahal? I know who built it. Shah Jahan.

MARGARET: The favorite wife was Mumtaz Mahal.

KATHARINE: Mumtaz, of course! It was on the tip of my tongue.

MARGARET: It took twenty-two years and twenty thousand workers to build.

KATHARINE: Is this going to be some sort of pop quiz?

MARGARET: I was trying to get your mind off Walter.

KATHARINE: Nothing will ever get my mind off Walter.

MARGARET: This is a wonderful start to a trip!

KATHARINE: I'm sorry. (*She hums a little.*)

MARGARET: Kitty, sshh!, you're doing it. It's nobody's fault.

(KATHARINE *begins to read from a travel brochure she has taken out of her purse.*)

KATHARINE: Now listen to this. (*She reads.*) "Don't drink the water, which means absolutely no ice in your drinks or eating of washed fruit and vegetables." Sounds charming. "Above all be patient. Allow, accept, be."

MARGARET: That's what I've been telling you.

(*A light comes up on* GANESHA. *He is sitting on the wing. He wears a leather flight jacket and an aviator's white silk scarf which blows wildly in the rushing wind we can suddenly hear. He waves to* KATHARINE.)

KATHARINE (*suddenly*): What's that out there?

MARGARET: Oh, my God! Out where?

KATHARINE: Out there, on the wing!

MARGARET: I don't want to know.

KATHARINE: Margaret, look!

MARGARET: I don't want to look.

KATHARINE: There's nothing wrong. There's something wonderful. It's beautiful. Just look.

(MAN *appears. He is an* AGING HIPPIE. *He leans over* MARGARET *to look out the window.*)

MAN: What's happening? We on fire? Oh, wow!

MARGARET: Do you mind!

KATHARINE: Do you see what I see?

MAN: We don't get shit like this at the back of the plane.

KATHARINE: It looks like an angel. Do you believe in angels?

MAN: Lady, I believe in everything.

MARGARET: If you'd like me to get up, so you two can continue this—

MAN: I was just on my way to the head. You want to see some real fucking angels, pardon the expression, check out the caves in Ajanta. Angels and red monkeys. I didn't believe in shit till I checked out Ajanta.

KATHARINE: Ajanta? Is that on our itinerary, Margaret?

MARGARET: You know it is. Thank you.

MAN: Okay, okay, lady. You made your point. I'm going back to peasant class.

MARGARET: I didn't say a word.

MAN: You didn't have to. It was in the eyes. It's always in the eyes. You have cruel eyes. They're filled with hate. I mean that nicely. I mean that sincerely.

KATHARINE: Now just a minute.

MAN: Your friend needs a good purge in the Ganges. I don't think she's ready for Katmandu yet. There's not enough dope in the Himalayas to mellow that dude out.

(*He goes.*)

MARGARET: I hate it when they do that. The first-class bathrooms should be for the first-class passengers.

KATHARINE: Do you want me to make a citizen's arrest? Relax, Margaret.

MARGARET: When did you get so serene?

KATHARINE: I took a pill.

MARGARET: I don't know why they bother to have classes if they're not going to enforce them.

KATHARINE: You don't have cruel eyes.

MARGARET: Thank you.

KATHARINE: You have beautiful eyes. Don't cry.

MARGARET: I'm not crying. Does it look like I'm crying? (*She puts her headset back on.*)

KATHARINE: People like that don't know what they're saying half the time. That, or they speak before they think. Don't mind them. I've always liked your eyes.

MARGARET: I'm fine, Kitty. I'm trying to watch the movie!

(KATHARINE *watches her a moment, then puts her own headset back on.*)

(GANESHA *shakes his head and looks up from his newspaper.*)

GANESHA: Lord, Lord, Lord! Little Puck said it best: ''Shiva, what fools these mortals be!'' Such thoughtless, needless cruelty. Down there on earth, up here at forty-one thousand feet. (We went higher to avoid the turbulence while you weren't looking.) *We* are the ones who are powerless. We can only sigh and shake our heads. There's a serenity in being a god but very little real power. We gave it all to you.

KATHARINE: I choose to be happy. I choose to be loving. I choose to be good.

(*She will repeat this over and over.*)

   (*Tears are running down* MARGARET*'s cheeks as she watches the movie.*)

(MAN *appears on the wing of the plane. He is* WALTER. *His clothes are bloodied, his features battered from the beating that killed him.*)

GANESHA: Hello, Walter.

MAN: Mind if I join you out here?

GANESHA: I'd be honored.

MAN: I really have to draw the line at bad curry and movies about unrepentant heterosexuals.

GANESHA: Heterosexuals aren't so bad. Where would we be without them? Please.

(MAN *sits on the wing at* GANESHA*'s feet.*)

MAN: What are you?

GANESHA: I take whatever I can get. I'm speaking about affection. Physical love was never my strong suit. I'm not that sort of god. Fag?

(*He offers* MAN *a cigarette.*)

   I'm sorry. The raj is over but the melody lingers on! The Hindi word for tobacco is *nanded.*

MAN: *Nanded*, that's a nice word. Well, nicer than "fag."

(*They will smoke.*)

GANESHA: I thought that was you when we were boarding.

MAN: Where my mother goes, can this one be far behind? Listen, India has got to beat another of her annual same old two weeks in the Caribbean with the Civils.

GANESHA: Mrs. Civil is inconsolable. You must have heard what happened.

MAN: It served her right.

GANESHA: Look at her. I hate to see a woman cry.

MAN: I don't like Mrs. Civil. Mrs. Civil didn't like me. Let her cry her stone-cold heart out. Mrs. Civil was a bitch. Is. Is a bitch. I'm the "was."

GANESHA: Your words are like daggers, Walter. They cause me such pain.

MAN: Different people sing from different charts, old man.

GANESHA: Not half so old and hard as you.

KATHARINE: I choose to be happy. I choose to be loving. I choose to be good.

GANESHA: Your mother's been thinking about you again.

MAN: I'd like her to stop. I'd like her to forget all about me.

GANESHA: There will never come that day. She loves you. You're her son.

MAN: That's not love. It's guilt that's become a curse. She should have loved me not just for falling down and scraping my knee when I was a little boy but for standing tall when I was a young man and telling her I loved other men. She should have loved me when my heart was breaking for the love of them. She should have loved me when I wanted to tell her my heart was finally, forever full with someone— Jonathan!—but I didn't dare. She should have loved me the most when he was gone, that terrible day when my life was over.

(KATHARINE *has taken off her headset and she will be drawn into the scene.*)

KATHARINE: I choose to be happy. I choose to be loving. I choose to be good.

MAN: Instead you waited. You waited until late one night, I was coming home—no! to our "apartment," as you always put it; "Two men can't have a 'home,' Walter"—maybe I had a little too much to drink, certainly a lot too much pain and anger to bear—

KATHARINE: I didn't know.

MAN: A car whizzes by. Voices, young voices, scream the obligatory epithets: "Fag. Queer. Cocksucker. Dead-from-AIDS queer meat."

GANESHA: Oh dear, oh dear!

MAN: I make the obligatory Gay Nineties gesture back. (*He gives the finger.*) Die from my cum, you assholes!

GANESHA: Oh dear, oh dear!

MAN: The car stops. The street is empty. Suddenly this part seems obligatory, too. Six young men pile out.

KATHARINE: Black! All of them black!

MAN: No, mother! All of them you!

MARGARET (*loudly, because of the headset*): I think we saw this movie at Watch Hill!

MAN: Six young men with chains and bats. One had a putter.

KATHARINE: Six young black men! Hoodlums! Two of them had records!

GANESHA: Oh, dear! Oh, dear! All of you!

MAN: I stood there. It seemed like it took them forever to get to where I was standing. There was a funny silence. Probably because I wasn't scared. I said "Hello." I don't know why. I hated them. I hated everything about them. I hated what they were going to do to me. I knew it would hurt. I wanted it to be quick. I didn't want them to know I was afraid. So I said "Hello" again. The one with the putter swung first. You could hear the sound. Whoosh. Ungh! against the side of my head. I could feel the skull cracking. He'd landed a good one. Then they all started swinging and beating and kicking. I stayed on my feet a remarkably long time. I was sort of proud of me. Finally I went down and they kept on swinging and beating and kicking, only now it wasn't hurting so much. It was more abstract. I could *watch* the pain, corroborate it. Finally, they got back in their car, not speaking anymore. They weren't having such a good time either anymore, I guess. None of us were. I was just lying there, couldn't move, couldn't speak, when I could hear their car screeching a U-turn and it coming towards me, real fast, just swerving at the last minute, only missing my head by about this much. What I figure is this: they were gonna run me over but at the last second one of them grabbed the wheel. So they weren't one hundred percent animal. One of them had a little humanity. Just a touch. Maybe. If my theory's right, that is. But that's when you waited to love me, Mama.

KATHARINE: I always loved you.

MAN: That's when you waited to know it.

KATHARINE: Why are you doing this?

MAN: Let me go. Let us both go.

KATHARINE: I can't. You're my firstborn.

MAN: There's Pop. There's Jerry. There's Sis and the kids.

KATHARINE: You were my favorite.

MAN: You were mine. We killed each other.

KATHARINE: Where's your scarf? You'll catch a chill without your scarf.

MAN: You sound like Jonathan.

KATHARINE: Give me a kiss.

MAN: No, I don't want to kiss you.

KATHARINE: You will. (*She puts her headset back on.*)

MAN: Pop! I never called Dad "Pop" in my entire life! It must
be the altitude.

(*He goes.* MARGARET *takes off her headset in disgust with the
movie. She has stopped crying.*)

MARGARET: And they all lived happily ever after. Sure they did.

(*She sees that* KATHARINE *is crying now. She takes her hand
soothingly.*)

It's all right. It's all right.

KATHARINE: I choose to be happy. I choose to be loving. I choose
to be good.

(*Lights begin to fade on the two women.*)

GANESHA: Oh dear, oh dear! Let's go to India!

(*He claps his hands twice.*)

(*Music. The sound of the jet engines will fade away and all we
will hear are the delicate sounds of a wooden flute.*)

(GANESHA *has pulled down a map of the subcontinent.*)

GANESHA: India, a republic in South Asia; comprises most of
former British India and the semi-independent Indian states
and agencies; became a dominion in 1947; became fully
independent on January 26, 1950, with membership in the
British Commonwealth of Nations. Population as of the last
census, 813 million. Area: 1,246,880 square miles. Principal
language: Hindi. I was born right here. Kerala. The most
beautiful part of India. The beaches alone. The temples at

Tiruchchirappalli (trust me, but don't ask me to spell it). How I was born is a very interesting story. Some say I was created out of a mother's loneliness. Some say I was the expression of a woman's deepest need. I say: I don't know. What child does?

SCENE THREE

MAN *appears. He is a* PORTER *at the Bombay airport. He has Katharine's and Margaret's luggage on a dolly.*

KATHARINE: Wait! Stop! Stop right there! Come back with those.

GANESHA: Excuse me. They've landed and things are getting quite out of hand at the Bombay airport.

KATHARINE: I had eight pieces. Something is missing. One, two, three . . . !

MARGARET: Where's the guide? They said he'd be waiting with a sign with our names on it.

KATHARINE: There's only seven now. I know I had eight.

MARGARET: When we got off the plane, they said he'll meet you at customs. At customs, they said he'll meet you just outside customs. Now we're outside customs and there's not even someone to tell us the next place he's not going to meet us!

KATHARINE: I know what's missing: my cassette player with all my tapes. All my Frank Sinatra and Mozart and Cole Porter. This is terrible. Do you speak English, young man? Do you understand? He doesn't speak English.

(GANESHA *steps forward to greet them. He is wearing a blazer.*)

Mrs. Alan Civil? Mrs. George Brynne?

MARGARET: Thank God!

GANESHA: You're welcome, Mrs. Civil. Just a little joke.

KATHARINE: And you are?

GANESHA: Your representative from Red Carpet Tours. I have a car and driver waiting for you at the curb. Your suite at the Taj Palace is in order. You have a most excellent view of the harbor and the Gate of India. Come.

KATHARINE: I'm missing something. A cassette player and all my tapes.

GANESHA: Did you take her cassette player?

MAN: What do you think?

GANESHA: I think you should give it back to her.

MAN: Get lost, Pop.

GANESHA: Is this the impression you want our country to make?

MAN: Well, it's a little more honest than yours. "You have a most excellent view of the harbor and Gate of India." I'll show the ladies a most excellent view of my ass.

KATHARINE: What are they saying?

MARGARET: I don't speak Hindi, Kitty.

KATHARINE: Why are you snapping at me?

MARGARET: I've been up for a day and a half on a plane. I'd like to get to our hotel.

KATHARINE: So would I.

MARGARET: I don't know why this should call for a big discussion. What's he saying?

GANESHA: He says he will check the lost and found and bring your player to the hotel if it is returned.

KATHARINE: "Returned?" That means someone took it!

GANESHA: I meant "found." I translated badly.

(MAN *starts wheeling the luggage off on his dolly.*)

KATHARINE: Where's he going?

GANESHA: Not to worry. I told him to start loading the boot.

KATHARINE: That's it for the cassette player? Don't I get a receipt, a claim check or something?

GANESHA: Leave everything to me.

MARGARET: What do you want him to do, Katharine? Mrs. Brynne is a loser. I mean, she loses things. That came out badly in translation, too.

GANESHA: Come. India and a soft bed await you.

KATHARINE: Just a minute. I want to take all this in.

MARGARET: What is there to take in, Kitty? It's an airport.

(KATHARINE *doesn't budge.* MARGARET *sighs audibly.*)

Hurry up if you're going to do that. (*To* GANESHA:) Mrs. Brynne is also something of an enthusiast.

(MARGARET *and* GANESHA *start walking off.* KATHARINE *will remain.*)

GANESHA: What would you like to know about Bombay?

MARGARET: Nearly everything but not right now. I'm too tired.

GANESHA: It's very big, Bombay.

MARGARET: So was China.

(*They are gone.*)

KATHARINE: "O for a Muse of fire!" I'm not going to let a missing cassette player spoil this. The world is filled with ill-manufactured cassette players from Taiwan but only one me, Katharine Brynne, née Mitchell, born too many years ago in a ridiculous place when I consider to where I've come, experiencing this one particular and special moment. Look. Attack things with your eyes. See them fiercely. Listen. Hear everything, ignore nothing. Smell. Breathe deeper than you've ever dared. Experience. Be. But above all, remember. Carve adamantine letters in your brain: "This I have seen and done and known." Amen. No, above all, *feel*! Take my heart and do with it what you will.

(*She takes a long look at the terminal.*)

Yes.

(*Lights change to make transition to next scene, but* KATHARINE *stays where she is.*)

(*Music.*)

(GANESHA *appears.*)

GANESHA: There are three people you must know about in my story.

(*He pulls down a chart with the appropriate pictures.*)

My mother, Parvati (isn't she lovely?), my father, Shiva, and me. One day, before I was born, my mother, Parvati, was sitting in her bath. She told an attendant to let no one enter, not even Shiva, her lord and master. But Shiva is everyone's lord and master, and no one dared stop him from entering his wife's bath. Parvati covered herself in shame, she had no prestige now, but she was angry, too. Some say she decided then and there she must have a gana of her own. A gana is someone obedient to our will and our will alone. No woman had ever had a gana of her own. This is what happened: my mother, Parvati, gathered the saffron paste from her own body and with her own hand created a boy, her firstborn, her gana, me! Oh, how lovely it is to be born! We were so happy!

(*Lights have changed. We are in a hotel room.*)

SCENE FOUR

A hotel room with an overhead fan and a balcony. MARGARET *is reading from a guide book.* KATHARINE *is listening to* GANESHA.

MARGARET: I'm a little worried how we're going to handle your poverty, Mr. Vitankar.

KATHARINE: Maggie, please, we're right in the middle of something important.

MARGARET: I thought he was finished.

KATHARINE: I'm sorry, Mr. Vitankar.

GANESHA: It's quite all right. I'm sure you'll be handling it very well indeed, Mrs. Civil. Your poverty is angry. Ours is not. In India, poverty is not an emotion. It's a fact.

MARGARET: What about the status of women in India?

GANESHA: The lot of women in India is very, very dismal. We set you on fire when you don't obey and expect you to set yourselves on fire to show proper mourning when we die. Does that answer your question?

MARGARET: I think so.

KATHARINE: That's dreadful.

GANESHA: But we're a democracy now. That's the main thing to know about us. The largest democracy in the world. So maybe there's hope for you ladies yet. Change things. Vote. Tell us men where to go. You're very tired. We'll continue the story of Lord Ganesh tomorrow.

KATHARINE: You have so many gods! Keeping them straight! Vishnu, Parvati, Ganesh! He sounds like a Jewish food.

GANESHA: No offense, but Lord Ganesha is better than a bagel.

KATHARINE: We're not offended. We're not Jewish.

GANESHA: Tomorrow morning then? Eight o'clock.

(MAN *is now a* PORTER. *He carries a tray with two Coca-Colas.*)

    The ladies asked for Diet Pepsi.

MARGARET: That's all right.

MAN: The ladies are fortunate to get anything at this hour.

GANESHA: You are a very rude waiter, young man.

MAN: We're a union now. I don't have to be polite anymore.

GANESHA: He said the hotel is out of Diet Pepsi and a million apologies.

MARGARET: It's a wonderful language. It almost sounds like Japanese.

MAN: What is she saying?

GANESHA: She agrees. You're a very rude waiter, young man. Shame on you.

MAN: Shame on me? Shame on you. These are Jew Christian old whores with white saggy skin. Their shit is on your tongue from all the ass licking. You are no Indian. You are no one. Tell them in your perfect English that I'm waiting for my tip. For another twenty rupees I will fuck them.

MARGARET: See what I mean, Kitty? It's more the rhythm than the sound of Japanese.

(GANESHA *gives* MAN *a tip.*)

MAN: Thank you, Papa India. Thank you, *babu*. I smile at the ladies. I exit the room backwards and bowing. I wish the old bags a good night.

(*He smiles and is gone.*)

MARGARET: Thank you.

KATHARINE: *¡Muchas gracias!*

MARGARET: That smile! Those wonderful teeth against that wonderful dark skin! It's like ebony. No, mahogany! Are all Indian men such heartbreakers, Mr. . . . I'm sorry.

GANESHA: Mr. Vitankar.

(*The telephone rings.* KATHARINE *answers.*)

KATHARINE: Hello? Hello?

MARGARET: Till tomorrow then, Mr. Vitankar. Good night.

GANESHA (*taking his leave*): Mrs. Civil, Mrs. Brynne.

KATHARINE (*still into phone*): Hello? (*To* GANESHA:) Goodbye! *¡Gracias! ¡Muchas gracias!*

GANESHA: *De nada.*

KATHARINE (*back into phone*): Hello? There's no one there.

GANESHA: Now you're truly in India.

(*He bows, backs himself out of the room, much as the* MAN/PORTER *did.*)

MARGARET: Really, Katharine!

KATHARINE: What?

MARGARET: That is so patronizing!

KATHARINE: What is?

MARGARET: Speaking Spanish to an Indian. What is that? Your generic Third World "thank you"?

KATHARINE: I'm sorry, but I don't know the word for "thank you" in Hindi.

MARGARET: Well, it isn't *gracias*!

KATHARINE: He knew what I meant.

MARGARET: He would have known what you meant in your native language. *Gracias* reduces him to the level of a peon and you to that of a horrid tourist.

KATHARINE: My intention was to thank him, Margaret. On that level I think my *gracias* was highly effective. Now, which bed would you like?

MARGARET: It's really of no interest to me.

KATHARINE: I wish you would adopt such a generous attitude towards me. I'll take this one then. I hope you remembered the alarm clock. That was your responsibility!

(*They have begun to unpack.*)

MARGARET: I'm sorry, but if we're going to travel together you've got to understand something about me. I am very sensitive to the feelings of others.

KATHARINE: You could have fooled me.

MARGARET: Frankly, you've said and done several things that have offended me since we got on the plane. No, "offended" is too strong a word. Let's say "embarrassed." There! I've said it and I'm glad. The air is cleared.

KATHARINE: Don't stop now, Margaret, I'm all ears.

MARGARET: You're sure?

KATHARINE: Absolutely! If we're going to "travel together" for the next two weeks, let's have absolute candor. I hate that outfit.

MARGARET: Be serious! That remark about Jewish food just now. I could have died. Comparing one of their gods to a bagel.

KATHARINE: He compared him to a bagel. I only said he sounded like something Jewish you ate.

MARGARET: Will you keep your voice down?

KATHARINE: No! And stop saying that. I am sick and tired of being told to keep my voice down when I am not in the wrong. And even if I were in the wrong, you have no business telling me to keep my voice down. I am not your cowed daughter or your catatonic husband and I am not about to become your cowed and catatonic traveling companion. I'm me. You're you. Respect the difference or go home. I came to India to have an adventure. This is not an adventure. This is the same old Shinola.

MARGARET: Well, it's nice to know what your best friend really thinks of you. And your family.

KATHARINE: I didn't mean that. I'm very fond of Joy. And Alan's just quiet around us. I'm sure he's quite talkative when you two are alone.

MARGARET: Not especially.

KATHARINE: I'll give you ''O for a Muse of fire.'' I probably do it just to annoy you, like you and the Lalique.

MARGARET: Every time you say it, I say to myself ''O for someone who didn't say 'O for a Muse of fire' at the drop of a hat.''

KATHARINE: It wouldn't bother me if you did.

MARGARET: Well, that's the difference between us.

KATHARINE: If you can't respect it, at least observe it.

MARGARET: You've changed. Ever since you went to those lectures in Bridgeport. ''Nurturing Your Inner Child''! You know what I say? Stifle him! If we all nurtured our inner child, Katharine, this planet would come to a grinding halt while we all had a good cry.

KATHARINE: Well, maybe it should.

(*There is a pause. They are each lost in their own particular thoughts. When they take a breath and sigh, it will be together.*)

MARGARET: "O for a Muse of fire" is right! Bartender! One fiery muse, a decent analyst, and an extra-dry gin martini.

KATHARINE: Don't say that. I think it's wonderful what you've done. I couldn't have done it.

MARGARET: I finally know what "the skin of your teeth" means. It's a layer you don't want to be involved with. Anyway, I'm sorry I let it get under my skin. Not you, "it."

KATHARINE: It's Shakespeare. "Muse of fire."

MARGARET: I know that. That is so patronizing, to tell me it's Shakespeare!

KATHARINE: I didn't know it until they showed it on Public Television. It's the first line of *Henry V*. How hard it is to really describe anything. And I have that trouble, don't you?

MARGARET: I don't know. Probably.

KATHARINE: "Muse of fire" is my talisman. It's my way of telling myself, "Savor this moment, Katharine Brynne née Mitchell. Relish it. It is important. You'll never be here or feel this way again."

MARGARET: This is what I mean. Those lectures in Bridgeport.

KATHARINE: That's not nurturing my inner child. It's Shakespeare. Telling you you can be a pain in the ass is nurturing my inner child.

MARGARET: Now I'm a pain in the ass!

(*They have finished unpacking and will now begin to make ready for bed.*)

KATHARINE: I didn't say you were a pain in the ass. I said you could be a pain in the ass. I'm hoping the next two weeks you won't be.

(*The phone begins to ring. This time* MARGARET *will answer it.*)

MARGARET: I have never been a pain in the ass for two entire weeks. Have I? (*Into phone:*) Hello?

KATHARINE: That's right, we were only in Barbados for eleven days.

MARGARET: Blame that trip on Barbados, not me! Hello?

KATHARINE: Everyone's toilet was broken.

MARGARET: Seven years later she throws Barbados in my face! Hello? (*She hangs up.*) There's no one there.

KATHARINE: I hope you haven't come to India for their telephones *or* the plumbing!

MARGARET: There you go again! Patronizing! I've come to India for personal reasons. Just as you've come for yours.

KATHARINE: I thought we came to India for a vacation.

MARGARET: I adore you, Kitty, even when you're impossible.

KATHARINE: No, you don't. I don't think we are best friends. I don't think we know each other at all.

MARGARET: I'm sorry you feel that way. I feel very warmly towards you.

KATHARINE: I know. Me, too.

MARGARET: It's going to be fine. From this moment on, we're going to get along famously and become the very best of friends.

KATHARINE: Who says?

MARGARET: My inner child. Do you mind if I nip in the loo first?

KATHARINE: Where do you think we are, luv, the Dorchester?

(MARGARET *goes into the bathroom area of their hotel room.*)

We have a balcony. Did you know we had a balcony? We have two of them! (*She steps forward onto the balcony.*)

MARGARET: How does the rest of it go? Do you know? "O for a muse of fire" *what*?

(KATHARINE *stands looking at the harbor in front of the hotel. She is overwhelmed by what she sees.*)

KATHARINE:

"O for a Muse of fire, that would ascend
The brightest heaven of invention!"

(MARGARET *screams in the bathroom.*)

MARGARET: Don't mind me. It's only a waterbug the size of a standard poodle.

KATHARINE:

"A kingdom for a stage, princes to act,
And monarchs to behold the swelling scene!"
Well, something like that.

(*The* MAN *has appeared on an adjoining balcony. He is* HARRY, *a young man.*)

MAN: Very good.

KATHARINE: Hello.

MAN: Hi. Fairly spectacular, isn't it? Especially this time of al-most-morning, not-quite-dawn. We couldn't sleep.

KATHARINE: We just got in.

MAN:

> "Then should the warlike Harry, like himself,
> Assume the port of Mars; and at his heels,
> Leashed in like hounds, should famine, sword, and fire
> Crouch for employment."

KATHARINE: Very good yourself!

MAN: I have no idea what it means: "Crouch for employment"?

KATHARINE: I like the sound of it!

MAN: And I did that part! I wore red tights and everyone said I had terrific legs. No one mentioned my performance.

KATHARINE: You're an actor?

MAN: For one brief shining hour in college. I'm a doctor. Or I was. I'm sick now. A physician who cannot heal himself.

KATHARINE: I'm sorry.

MAN:

> "But pardon, gentles all,
> The flat unraisèd spirits that hath dared
> On this unworthy scaffold to bring forth
> So great an object." Deedle-diddle-dee.
> You've got to help me here.

KATHARINE:

> "Can this cockpit hold
> The vasty fields of France? Or may we cram
> Within this wooden O—"
> That's my favorite part.

MAN: Me, too. "This wooden O"!

KATHARINE: "Within this wooden O the very casques"—

MAN (*very loud and heroic*): "That did affright the air at Agincourt?" (*His last words ring in the night air.*)

MARGARET: Kitty? What's going on out there?

MAN (*over his shoulder*): Okay, we'll keep it down, Ben. Sorry. (*To* KATHARINE:) He's got his hands full with this one.

KATHARINE: So does Mrs. Civil.

MAN: You're traveling with someone you call Mrs. Civil? This is very Tennessee Williams, or very Dickensian, I can't decide which.

KATHARINE: Well, I don't call her Mrs. Civil. Her name is Margaret. I'm Katharine, Kate, Kitty—I've been called everything. I prefer Katharine.

MAN: Hello, Katharine. I'm Harry.

KATHARINE: Katharine Brynne.

MAN: Harold Walter Strong.

KATHARINE: I had a son named Walter.

MAN: I'm sorry.

KATHARINE: Me, too.

MAN: How long has it been?

KATHARINE: Three years, feels like yesterday. Is that the Gate of India?

MAN: It was built for Queen Victoria's Jubilee visit to her prize colony. She never came. I guess she had something better to do. The British have a real attitude problem when it comes to anyone else, especially wogs (their not-so-nice word for people of a certain color). God knows, they loathe us. (I'm assuming you're a Yank.) All that "luv" and "darling" and "Ta ta, duckie" and they hate our guts. Ask me how I know all this? Did I spend a term at Oxford? No. Did I rent rooms for the season in Belgravia? No. I'm talking off the top of my head. It's just a feeling I have. I'll shut up and watch the sun rise over Bombay Harbor with you.

(*By now we should be aware that* KATHARINE *is humming again.*)

What's that you're humming?

KATHARINE: Oh, nothing, I'm sorry.

MAN: "Blow the Wind Southerly," right?

KATHARINE: I don't know.

MAN: It is. I love that song. (*He begins to sing.*)

KATHARINE: Please. Don't. I couldn't bear it. It was my son's favorite song.

MAN: I understand. I'll tell him he had good taste in music and mothers.

KATHARINE: Don't talk like that.

(GANESHA *comes out on the terrace with* MAN.)

GANESHA: You're barefoot. Where are your slippers? And your robe! You're drenched. Jesus! You're soaking wet.

MAN: This is Ben, Katharine. He worries about me. That's all right, I worry about him. We're neither of us terribly well.

GANESHA: Hello, Katharine. Excuse me. You're burning up.

MAN: I'm freezing, actually!

(MARGARET *comes out of the bathroom area of their room. She is brushing her teeth.*)

MARGARET: It's all yours, Kitty!

(*She will go out onto another balcony off their hotel room.*)

GANESHA: I'll get your robe.

MAN: I can do it.

(*They exit,* GANESHA *supporting* MAN.)

MARGARET: I said it's all yours. I picked up Crest gel instead of their toothpaste. I'm always doing that. I think they make the boxes almost identical just to confuse people. I hate gel. It sticks to my fingers. I guess that's the Gate of India, Bombay Harbor, and the Indian Ocean beyond. I guess we're here. We're really, really here. What is all that down there, Kitty? In the square, the plaza, in front of the hotel and all around the Gate? It's like something moving.

KATHARINE: It's people sleeping.

MARGARET: It's too dense for people.

KATHARINE: It's people.

MARGARET: Then it's all people. There's no place we're seeing the pavement then. Wall-to-wall people.

KATHARINE: I think it's beautiful.

MARGARET: I'm sure they don't. Excuse me, I've got to spit again.

(*She goes back to bathroom area.*)

KATHARINE (*singing, softly, to herself*):

"Blow the wind southerly, southerly, southerly
Blow the wind south o'er the bonny blue sea.
Blow the wind southerly, southerly, southerly
Blow, bonny breeze, my lover to me."

(*She has trouble continuing.* GANESHA *has appeared on an adjoining balcony.*)

"They told me last night there were ships in the offing
And I hurried down to the deep rolling sea.

But my eye could not see it, wherever might be it,
The bark that is bearing my lover to me.''

GANESHA: Don't stop.

KATHARINE: I'm sorry. I should have realized. Everyone's doors are open.

GANESHA: My wife said, ''Listen, Toshiro. Listen, an angel is singing.''

KATHARINE: I'm hardly an angel, I have the voice of a frog and truly, I didn't mean to wake you.

GANESHA: Why are you crying, Mrs. Brynne?

KATHARINE: I'm not crying.

GANESHA: May I assuage your tears?

KATHARINE: I said, I'm not crying.

GANESHA: I would like to help you.

KATHARINE: How do you know my name?

GANESHA: We were going through customs. I see I made very little impression. Permit me to introduce myself again. Toshiro Watanabe of Nagasaki. My wife is Yuriko.

KATHARINE: If you say so.

GANESHA: Be careful of India, Mrs. Brynne. Be very careful here. If you're not, you may find yourself here.

KATHARINE: You sound like someone in a very bad novel or movie or play about India.

GANESHA: Lord knows we've had our fill of them!

KATHARINE: I came to India because I didn't want to go to some mindless resort in the Caribbean with our two husbands for the ninetieth year in a row and the children and the in-laws and the cats and the dogs and the turtles are all out of the house or dead or married and no one is especially depending on me right now. This is my turn.

GANESHA: Why India?

KATHARINE: Why not?

GANESHA: Why not the Grand Canyon? Why not Niagara Falls? Why not Disneyland? Why India?

KATHARINE: I heard it could heal. And now I sound like someone in a very bad novel or movie.

GANESHA: What part of you needs healing, Mrs. Brynne?

KATHARINE: I thought you Japanese were very circumspect. You go right for the jugular, Mr. —

GANESHA: Watanabe. I am one singular Nipponese, Mrs. Brynne!

(MAN *is heard off calling to* GANESHA.)

MAN: Toshiro!

GANESHA (*over his shoulder*): I'm coming, Buttercup, I'm coming! (*To* KATHARINE:) You think it is only your heart that is broken. May I be so bold as to suggest it is your soul that is crying out in this Indian dawn? Hearts can be mended. Time can heal them. But souls . . . ! Tricky, tricky business, souls. I wish you well. You've come to the right place. *Ciao,* Mrs. Brynne, *sayonara.*

(*He goes.* MARGARET *returns. She is in a nightgown. She goes to "her" adjoining balcony.*)

MARGARET: Sorry I took so long. I . . .

KATHARINE: What?

MARGARET: Never mind. It's all yours for good now.

KATHARINE: This view is extraordinary. See? They are people. Thousands and thousands and thousands of people.

MARGARET: More like hundreds, Kitty. Dreadful! Well, don't say they didn't warn us. We were warned!

KATHARINE: Extraordinary!

MARGARET: I thought I heard voices out here. Were you talking to someone?

KATHARINE: Our neighbor, one very outspoken Jap.

MARGARET: Oh my God, I hope you didn't call him that, Kitty! To his face!

KATHARINE: I don't remember.

MARGARET: They're not Japs, you don't call them Japs anymore, the war is over! They're Japanese. You're going to start an international incident.

KATHARINE: I think I called him an Oriental.

MARGARET: That's just as bad. It's worse. "Oriental" conjures up flying carpets, Scheherazade, and chop suey.

KATHARINE: Whatever I called him, he didn't seem to mind.

MARGARET: Then he was being polite. Everyone minds being called something.

KATHARINE: Can we just enjoy this?

MARGARET: We should be sleeping.

KATHARINE: I'm too excited to sleep. Let's go down there.

MARGARET: What? Are you mad? Do you know what time it is?

KATHARINE: I just want to walk among them. Experience them.

MARGARET: You can experience them from up here.

KATHARINE: Don't you feel drawn to be a part of all that?

MARGARET: No.

KATHARINE: Come with me. Before it gets light. They won't know we're tourists.

MARGARET: I'm not dressed.

KATHARINE: I'm scared to do it alone.

MARGARET: I'd be scared to do it with an army. You can't just throw yourself into a mob of homeless, dirty, disease-ridden beggars your first hour here, Kitty.

KATHARINE: Who says?

MARGARET: What if there are lepers down there?

KATHARINE: I hope there are. Yes or no?

MARGARET: No.

KATHARINE: I'll wave up at you.

(*She goes.*)

MARGARET: Katharine!

(*Almost at once the phone begins to ring.* MARGARET *answers.*)

Hello? Hello?

(*She hangs the phone up.*)

(*She goes back onto the balcony.* GANESHA *has come back onto an adjoining balcony. He is wearing a colorful silk kimono.*)

GANESHA: My husband said you were upset. May I be of help?

MARGARET: Your husband was talking to my traveling companion, Mrs. Brynne.

GANESHA: Ah! And you? What about you?

MARGARET: I'm fine. No, I'm not. That's a beautiful wrap.

GANESHA: What's wrong?

MARGARET: I'm not very good at keeping an eye on people. They rush out into danger and I'm helpless to save them. I've just lost Mrs. Brynne in that still sleeping, just stirring crowd down there.

GANESHA: Your friend is in no physical danger.

MARGARET: Is there any other kind?

GANESHA: Yes. I heard you cry out in the bathroom. I'm sorry, but the air vents, I couldn't help but hear.

MARGARET: Oh, that! An enormous insect. I'm terrified of bugs. I'm sure the entire hotel heard me.

GANESHA: Twice you cried out. The second time was very soft. "Oh!" you went, just "Oh!"

MARGARET: There's a lump in my breast. I keep hoping it will go away. From time to time I touch it and it's always larger.

GANESHA: May I?

(MARGARET *allows* GANESHA *to touch her.*)

MARGARET: My first night in India and I'm allowing a strange woman in a gorgeous silk kimono that I covet—it's the other one—to touch my right breast. There you are. Home base. Feel it?

GANESHA: Oh!

MARGARET: You don't have to say anything.

GANESHA: Does your friend know?

MARGARET: She has enough troubles. We both do.

GANESHA: You're such a sad woman, Mrs. Civil. I'm so sorry.

MARGARET: Everyone thinks I'm a bossy bitch.

GANESHA: It's a clever defense.

MARGARET: I even fool Alan. Kitty's the one everyone loves. People like Kitty just have to be born to be loved. I've always had to work at it. I had my big chance and blew it. A son, my firstborn. His name was Gabriel. Such a beautiful name. Such a beautiful child. Gabriel. Never Gabe. Alan chose it. I used to love just saying it. Gabriel. Gabriel.

GANESHA: What happened?

MARGARET: I don't want to tell you. Where's Kitty? I don't see Kitty. We were in a park. Abingdon Square, Greenwich Village, in New York City. You wouldn't know it.

GANESHA: Where Bleecker and Hudson and Eighth Avenue all converge, just above Bank Street. Go on.

MARGARET: I'd just bought him a Good Humor bar. Maybe you know them, too?

GANESHA: Oh, yes; oh, yes! They're sclumptious!

MARGARET: His little face was covered with chocolate. I took a handkerchief out of my purse and wetted it with my tongue to clean his face. He pulled away from me. "No!" I pulled him back. "Yes!" Our eyes met. He looked at me with such hate . . . no! anger! . . . and pulled away again, this time hurting me. I rose to chase him, but he was off the curb and into the street and under the wheels of a car before I could save him. Isn't that what mothers are supposed to do? Save their children? His head was crushed. He was dead when I picked him up. I knew. I wouldn't let anyone else hold him. They say I carried him all the way to the hospital a few blocks away. I don't remember.

GANESHA: St. Vincent's. It's very famous. Dylan Thomas and Billie Holiday died there. I'm sorry.

MARGARET: He was four years old. Gorgeous blond curls I kept long—you could then. I think he would have grown up to be a prince among men.

GANESHA: All mothers do.

MARGARET: Do you have children?

GANESHA: No, and sometimes it is a great sadness to me. But only sometimes.

MARGARET: I don't know why I told you this. Strangers in the night. Scooby-dooby-doo.

GANESHA: No, new friends in the Indian dawn.

MARGARET: I've never told anyone about Gabriel. His brother and sister who came after. What would be the point? Alan and I never talk about it. This was years and years and years ago. We moved, we started a new family. I have another life. I wish I saw Kitty down there. The woman who drove the car was a black woman. We called them Negroes then. It wasn't her fault. She was devastated. I felt so sorry for her. During the service, Episcopalian, Alan's side of the family insisted, we're simple Methodist, we all heard a strange sound. Very faint at first.

(GANESHA *has begun to hum the spiritual "Swing Low, Sweet Chariot."*)

We weren't sure what we were hearing or if we were hearing anything at all. I thought it was the organ, but we hadn't asked for one. It was the Negro woman whose car had struck my son. She'd come to the funeral. I don't know how she heard about it. She was sitting by herself in a pew at the back. She was just humming, but the sound was so rich, so full, no wonder I'd thought it was the organ. The minister tried to continue, but eventually he stopped and we all just turned and listened to her. Her eyes were closed. Tears were streaming down her cheeks. Such a vibrant, comforting sound it was! Her voice rose, higher and higher, loud now, magnificent, like a bright shining sword. And then the words came.

(*She sings in a voice not at all like the one she has just described.*)

> "Swing low, sweet chariot,
> Comin' for to carry me home.
> Swing low, sweet chariot,
> Comin' for to carry me home."

(GANESHA *joins her.*)

> "Swing low, sweet chariot,
> Comin' for to carry me home.
> Swing low, sweet chariot,
> Comin' for to carry me home."

GANESHA: You're shivering. Here. Put this on. Lovely! It's yours.

(*He puts the kimono over her shoulders.*)

MARGARET: I couldn't.

GANESHA: Please, I insist.

MARGARET: It's not warranted, such kindness.

(*Lights come up on* KATHARINE *and* MAN *in a different part of the stage. They are "walking" down on the street as they talk. A turntable would be useful to accomplish this effect of walking and talking.*)

There she is!

KATHARINE: This is wonderful. Even more wonderful than I'd imagined. Sshh! We don't want to wake them. The light will do that soon enough. We have all this just to ourselves for a little while longer and then we'll disappear into it. Are you scared?

MAN: No. Am I nervous? Yes. Am I ready to run like hell back up to my room and Ben? You bet. Careful!

KATHARINE: I thought it was a—

MAN: It's a person.

KATHARINE: We must hold hands and we must never let go of each other.

MAN: It's a deal. Are you always so adventurous?

KATHARINE: Almost never. It's India.

GANESHA: That young man is going to die soon. So is his gentleman friend.

MARGARET: Must they?

GANESHA: Yes.

KATHARINE: Is this too fast for you?

MAN: Well, maybe a tad, Mrs. Brynne.

KATHARINE: You must call me Katharine and we shall be great friends forever and ever.

MAN: It's going to be a scorcher.

KATHARINE: Have you done Elephanta Island yet?

MAN: Our first day. Frankly, I was disappointed. They're Buddhist. I came to India for the Hindu stuff. Ben adored them. Of course, I fell, which didn't exactly help the festivities. Be careful getting off the ferry.

KATHARINE: Thank you. We will.

MARGARET (*to* GANESHA): Why must they die?

GANESHA (*with the slightest of shrugs*): Why not?

MAN: I'm afraid my Ben is going to be rather annoyed with you when he finds out I joined you down here in the madding crowd. He prefers to stay far from it. I've been dying to do this all week.

(*He looks up and sees* MARGARET *and* GANESHA *on the balconies looking down at them.*)

Look up there! We're being watched.

(*He calls up to* GANESHA.)

Good morning! Thank your husband for the cough syrup. It was very helpful.

KATHARINE: She can't hear you.

MARGARET: Kitty! Up here!

GANESHA: She can't hear you. Excuse me. I'm wanted elsewhere.

MARGARET: I can't accept this. You must let me give you something.

GANESHA: There's no need.

MARGARET: Do you smoke? I brought scads of cigarettes.

GANESHA: *Sayonara*, Mrs. Civil.

MARGARET: Goodbye.

(*He goes.* MARGARET *remains on balcony.*)

(*During the following, although the stage is almost bare, we will hear the sounds of many, many people. Dogs barking. Vendors. Intense crowds. India.*)

(KATHARINE *and* MAN *have reappeared on the street below Margaret's balcony.*)

KATHARINE: I don't believe it, Harry! Almost the first thing I see in India and it's a cliché. I asked for a Muse of fire and I get a bloody snake charmer!

MAN: Since when is a man in rags squatting on the pavement playing a wooden flute making a cobra coil out of a straw basket such a cliché for a lady from Connecticut? Can we stop a minute?

KATHARINE: I'm sorry. People probably think I'm your mother.

MAN: I'm sure my own mother wishes you were.

KATHARINE: What do you mean?

MAN: We don't get on. Let's keep walking. They're starting to wake up. You'll be getting the good ol' rope trick next!

KATHARINE: It serves me right. Thinking I would find India, experience it, my first morning here. But you see, Harry, I have a dream of this place, a dream of India.

MAN: I think we all do who come here, Katharine. Mine's easy. I want Ben and I to get well. If there's a choice, me first. I'm petty.

KATHARINE: No, you're not. My dream of India is this: that I am engulfed by it. That I am lost in a vast crowd such as this and become a part of it. That I'm devoured by it somehow, Harry.

MAN: I understand.

KATHARINE: It's a terrifying dream, but I have to walk through it. It's a dream of death, but purgation and renewal, too.

(*A light has come up on* GANESHA *sitting on the ground in a beggar's attitude. As* KATHARINE *moves toward him, the* MAN *will recede as she leaves him behind.*)

Look!

(GANESHA *takes off his elephant's head. It is the first time we have seen his face. He is a leper. He is hideous.*)

When I was a very young woman I wrote something in my diary that I've never wanted anyone to know until now.

This was before George. Before Walter. Before any of them. This is what I wrote, Harry.

(HARRY *is gone by now.*)

"Before I die, I want to kiss a leper fully on the mouth and not feel revulsion. I want to cradle an oozing, ulcerous fellow human against my breast and feel love. Katharine Mitchell."

(GANESHA *has opened his arms to her, half begging, half inviting her to come to him.*)

That's why I've come to India. I don't think I can do it, Harry.

(*She turns to him for support. He isn't there.*)

Harry? Harry?

MARGARET (*waving wildly*): Kitty, come up now! It's getting light!

KATHARINE: Harry, where are you? Oh God, if he's fallen somewhere in this crowd . . . Harry!

(*The sounds of India are getting louder and louder. It is the roar of a vast multitude, the tumult of humanity. It is more like a vibration than a sound. Ideally, we will all feel it as well as hear it.*)

MARGARET: Kitty! Look up here! I'm calling you!

KATHARINE: Harry! Please! Don't do this! Where are you?! Margaret!

MARGARET: She can't hear me. Something's wrong. Just come up now!

(KATHARINE *begins to blow on the whistle George gave her.*)

MARGARET: Kitty! Kitty! Kitty!

KATHARINE: Please, someone, help!

MARGARET: I can't hear you . . . Kitty, Kitty . . .

KATHARINE: I've lost someone, a young man, he's not well, he
    may have fallen.

(*She blows and blows the whistle, as* MARGARET *continues to
call down from the balcony.*)

(*The roaring is almost unendurable.*)

(GANESHA *claps his hands together. Once and all sounds stop.
Twice and the* OTHERS *all freeze. The third time and all the
lights snap off.*)

SCENE ONE

Another hotel room. The telephone is heard ringing wanly. We can also hear the sound of MARGARET *being sick in the bathroom off.* GANESHA *is working a carpet sweeper over a patch of very old, very thin rug. As he works, he watches a soap opera in Hindi on the television set. The* MAN *enters, using a pass key. He is carrying a tray of fresh fruit. He is the* HOTEL MANAGER.

MAN: Knock, knock.

GANESHA: Who's there?

MAN: Mahatma.

GANESHA: Mahatma who?

MAN: Mahatma Gandhi!

(*They roar with laughter.*)

GANESHA: Very good, Mr. Biswas, very droll! (*To us:*) Humor does not travel well. Especially Indian humor. "You had to be there" is, I believe, your word for it. Well, five words actually. You have to be here, I'm afraid.

MAN: What are you watching?

GANESHA: *The Ramayana*. It's very sad. Valmiki's wife is dying. She's sent for their firstborn to bless him before she dies. My husband says I cry at everything.

MAN: The actress playing her has fine breasts. Do you know what they call them in Boston? Jugs. The actress playing her has very fine jugs.

(*The phone stops ringing, but* MAN *picks it up anyway.*)

MAN: Hello? Hello? (*He hangs up.*) Bloody phone system. Bloody Third World. Bloody India. Why is it so dark in here? Are they here?

GANESHA: The nice one.

MAN: Mrs. Brynne?

GANESHA: Mrs. Civil.

MAN (*calling out*): Hello? *Bonjour? Guten Tag,* Mrs. Civil!

GANESHA: She's in the bathroom being sick.

MAN: That's how most of them see India. Staring at the bottom of a toilet bowl. Tell me, Mrs. Jog, would you fly halfway around the world and spend all your husband's money, just to heave your guts up for a fortnight in a country you have no way of understanding? I've seen this episode. It's a bloody rerun!

MARGARET (*off*): Yes? Is someone out there? Kitty? Is that you?

MAN: Some fruit, madam, compliments of the Lake Palace Hotel. Welcome to Udaipur!

MARGARET (*off*): What? I can't hear!

MAN: Let me open your shutters. You have a wonderful view here.

(*He throws open the shutters. Enormous light change. The gauze backdrop begins to sway in a delicious breeze coming in from the lake.*)

Lord, but it takes my breath away every time, Mrs. Jog! You can say bloody this and bloody that, Mr. Victor Biswas, but you can never say bloody *that*.

(MARGARET *comes into the room. She is in a robe and looks very pale.*)

MARGARET: Yes? Can I help you?

MAN (*singing, but not well*): "There she is, Miss America!" Welcome to the lake city of Udaipur, known as the City of the Sunrise, a cool oasis in the dry heart of Rajasthan, scene of a delightful episode in *Jewel in the Crown* and the exciting submarine/helicopter chase sequence in the most excellent James Bond motion picture *You Only Live Once.* Mr. Sean Connery himself occupied this very room.

MARGARET: Really!

GANESHA: *Twice. You Only Live Twice.*

MAN: Shut up. (*To* MARGARET:) The maid wants to know if she can get you anything?

MARGARET: No, thank you. I just want to be still for a little while. I'm a bit weak. It's so bright in here.

MAN: The way the sun hits the water. The Moghuls used to tie their prisoners to stakes and sew their eyelids open and make them look at the water until they went blind or mad or both.

MARGARET: How horrible!

MAN: We were conquered by a very cruel people. I hope you will find that very little of that cruelty remains. (*To* GA-NESHA:) What are you looking at?

GANESHA: I like hearing you speak English, Mr. Biswas. I am in awe of people who can speak with other people in a language not their own. That is a godlike thing to be able to do.

MAN (*to* MARGARET): The maid is saying she likes to hear me speak English. (*To* GANESHA:) Why? You don't understand. If you did, you would know I am telling this rich American lady what a lazy, worthless worker you are and that you are this close to being made redundant. Now clean room 617. Mr. Thomas had an accident on the sheets last night.

GANESHA: Please, don't make me redundant, Mr. Biswas. I need this job.

MAN: Then don't ever correct me again. Especially in front of a woman. (*To* MARGARET:) She's saying she hopes you enjoy your stay with us. Her name is Queenie.

MARGARET: Thank you, Queenie.

(GANESHA *heads for door just as* KATHARINE *returns.* KATHARINE *has been shopping. She has packages. She is out of breath but very excited.*)

KATHARINE: Offamof! Off-a-mof! Is that our view? (*She stands by the open window.*)

MAN: This is our very finest accomodation.

KATHARINE: Well, sir, as my grandchildren would say: OFF-A-FUCKING-MOF! The things I've seen and done this morning! You people have Bombay knocked into a cocked hat! (*To* MARGARET:) How are you feeling?

MARGARET: Much better.

KATHARINE: You sure? You had me worried. Poor baby.

MARGARET: This is Mr. Biswas, the hotel manager.

MAN: Victor Biswas. At your service, madam.

KATHARINE: Hello. I can see some color in her cheeks. Thank God! We have a train to catch this evening. (*She makes a quick Sign of the Cross.*) Whew! I've been shopping my tits off, Margaret. (*She finally sits.*)

MAN: Tits? Are they like jugs, Mrs. Brynne?

KATHARINE: I think they're a little more contemporary than jugs, Mr. Biswas.

MAN: I am also puzzling over your curious expression, "off-a-mof." The adjective you embellished it with I understood quite clearly.

KATHARINE: It's short for "O for a Muse of fire," which is Shakespeare and which I say when I get excited and can't describe things, and since I'm excited a lot lately, Mrs. Civil can't stand me saying it all the time and out of deference to her I shortened it to "offamof."

MAN: I see.

KATHARINE: "Thank you, Kitty." "*De nada,* Margaret." I didn't buy that much. It just looks like it. I spent fifty dollars, tops.

MAN: I hope you find everything you are looking for in our country, including good bargains. I come home burdened down with VCRs and Calvin Klein underwear whenever I visit yours. Excuse me. We have a busload of Japs arriving.

(*He goes.*)

KATHARINE: Did you hear that? He said "Japs."

MARGARET: He doesn't know better. Besides, it's not his first language.

KATHARINE (*to* GANESHA): Queenie, did you wash and iron my blouse?

GANESHA: Yes, Mrs. Brynne.

KATHARINE: *Ladesh.* (*To* MARGARET:) That's Hindi for "thank you." (*To* GANESHA:) *Ladesh,* Queenie, *ladesh.*

GANESHA: *De nada,* Mrs. Brynne.

(*He goes.*)

KATHARINE: Did you hear that, too, Margaret?

MARGARET: I heard, Kitty.

(KATHARINE *sticks her tongue out at her.*)

KATHARINE: I'm sorry. I couldn't resist. I'll shut up. It's the heat, I'm delirious, all this talk about Calvin Klein underwear! Do you want to see what I bought?

(*She will show her purchases to* MARGARET *during the following.*)

MARGARET: Kitty, what do you think a man like Mr. Biswas thinks when you say something like "shop your tits off"?

KATHARINE: I don't know. I don't care. I'm in India. I'm just your basic white trash, Margaret. You like these?

MARGARET: Don't be ridiculous.

KATHARINE: It's true. You are traveling with a woman whose father was a postal clerk and whose mother did ironing. I thought this blue bag would be for Linda Nagle.

MARGARET: Your father worked in a post office?

KATHARINE: For twenty-two years. He dropped dead selling Mrs. Feigen a three-cent stamp. Remember them? I was still in school. I did a little ironing myself after that. I think these are absolutely stunning, don't you? Only two dollars!

MARGARET: I had no idea, Kitty. Not that it matters.

KATHARINE: Oh, it matters, Margaret. Eventually, it matters. I have no class.

MARGARET: Don't say things like that.

KATHARINE: It's true.

MARGARET: Don't even think them. You and George have a wonderful life.

KATHARINE: I suppose we do, but it's not what I'm talking about. I think these will make darling luncheon napkins. You know how I met him? I crashed a dance at the Westchester Country Club. My best friend and I, Flo Sullivan, we made ourselves fancy evening dresses and hiked our skirts up and carried our shoes and we walked across the wet grass on the golf course and snuck into the party through the terrace. The ballroom was so beautiful! Roses everywhere. Real ones. A mirror ball. Guy Lombardo was playing. Himself, no substitute but the real thing. This was a class affair, right down the line. Guy Lombardo and His Royal Canadians. "Begin the Beguine." I knew right away this was where I wanted to be and I would do everything I could to stay there. I would scratch, I would fight, I would bite. Barbara Stanwyck was my role model. George was in white tie and tails, if you can imagine him in such a thing. He had a silver cigarette case and was tapping one end of his cigarette against it to get the tobacco down. I thought it was the most elegant gesture I'd ever seen a man make.

(*Lights up on* MAN. *He is* GEORGE, *dressed in white tie and tails and tapping a cigarette against a silver case. He will dance to the music* KATHARINE *has described.*)

We hit it off right away. I was a wonderful dancer. I'd made sure of that. I knew how to let the man think he was leading. With George I didn't have to. I knew he was going to ask me where I went to college. What I didn't know was what I was going to answer. When he did, it was during a lindy. I closed my eyes, held my breath, and jumped. "I graduated Port Chester High School and I'm working in the city as a dental assistant." "Great," he said. "I was afraid you were going to say you went to Vassar!" and laughed and lifted me up by the waist over his head for this incredibly long second, like we were two colored kids jitterbugging in Harlem, and I felt a blaze of happiness, like I've never felt before or since! After two hours, I said, "Let me wear your class ring. For fun. We'll pretend." It was a Yale ring. I showed it to Flo in the ladies' room during a band break. She couldn't believe it. She asked if she could try it on. I was washing my hands and it slipped out of my fingers and disappeared down the drain. What do you tell a man you just met two hours ago at a dance you crashed when you've lost his senior class ring? You don't tell him very much, Maggie. You sleep with him on the first date and you say "I do," after you make sure he asks you to bury him on the third. I mean, marry him. I can't believe I said that. Bury him. This is my favorite.

(*She is holding out a small carved figure.*)

MARGARET: What an extraordinary story. You never told me that.

KATHARINE: "Hi, I'm Katharine Brynne. I met my husband crashing a dance at the Westchester Country Club." I don't think so, Margaret. Do you know who that is? It's Ganesha.

(MARGARET *examines the carving. Lights up on* MAN. *He is* WALTER. *He is unbloodied.*)

MAN: May I have this dance, Miss Stanwyck? Oh, come on, it's only me. It's a slow fox trot. Your favorite kind. (*He holds his arms out to her.*)

KATHARINE: Since when do you like to dance with women?

MAN: I don't. I'll suffer.

(*She joins him.*)

Besides, you're not a woman. You're my mother.

(*They begin to dance. There is no music.*)

KATHARINE: Go ahead. Say it. Criticize. Everything I do is wrong.

MAN: How could you tell that story to a total stranger and not your own son?

KATHARINE: She's not a total stranger. Besides, you wouldn't have understood.

MAN: No, I would have understood. That's what you were afraid of. That's the kind of story that makes you like someone. We might have become friends over a story like that.

MARGARET: He—I guess it's a he; in this day and age, I better watch what I say—he/she/it's got the head of an elephant.

KATHARINE: You wouldn't have approved, Walter.

MAN: You think Mrs. Civil does? (*He laughs.*) God, I was a judgmental little shit where you and Dad were concerned.

KATHARINE: Serves us right. Well, me certainly. So am I still your best girl? Your *numero uno*?

MAN: I don't think we're supposed to say things like that.

KATHARINE: So sue me. That's from *Guys and Dolls*.

MAN: Shut up and dance. That's from *Gypsy*.

MARGARET: It looks like he's got four arms. I'm sure it's a he. Six arms? No, four. Definitely four.

MAN: This is a long song.

KATHARINE: We can stop.

MAN: I'm too much of a gentleman.

MARGARET: What's that around his waist? A snake! A cobra. And one of his tusks is broken.

(*Lights up on* GANESHA. *He is on a platform and holds his broken tusk in his right hand.*)

GANESHA: I broke it off one night and threw it at the moon because she made me angry by laughing at me.

KATHARINE: You still don't know how to hold a woman.

MAN: You mean, like this?

(*He pulls her to him hard and close.*)

Is this how you mean?

(*She slaps him.*)

KATHARINE: I'm sorry. I'm sorry.

MAN: No, you're not.

(MARGARET *approaches him.*)

MARGARET: May I cut in?

MAN: Thank you.

(*They begin to dance.*)

Do I know you?

MARGARET: No, Gabriel.

KATHARINE: Break her heart, the way you did mine. I hate you. I hate both of you!

MAN: Who are you?

MARGARET: Never mind. I just want to dance with you. I have always wanted to dance with you.

GANESHA (*to* KATHARINE): Join me. With worshippers at my feet I dance my swaying dance. Come, join us!

KATHARINE: Who are you?

GANESHA: I am Ganesha, a very important god in India. Don't laugh. Just because I'm fat and have the head of an elephant doesn't mean that I'm not a god of great influence and popularity. They call me the Lord of Obstacles. I am good at overcoming problems and bringing success to people. I am also known as a god of wisdom and wealth.

MARGARET: You're a wonderful dancer.

MAN: Thank you.

MARGARET: I'm not. You don't have to say anything.

MAN: I wasn't going to. Hang on!

(*This time he will whirl her wildly.*)

MARGARET: Oh, Gabriel!

(*They are gone.*)

KATHARINE: I think you're darling. Ganesh!

GANESHA: Or Ganesha. It's all the same to me.

KATHARINE: I like Ganesh. Tell me more. I want to know everything about you.

GANESHA: Because I'm a god, I don't have to look or do things the way ordinary people do. For instance, as you can plainly see, I have an elephant's head. You don't. You travel by Ford Escort or on foot. I ride a rat. It may seem strange for a great big fellow like me to have such a small vehicle, but I find him very helpful for getting out of tight situations. He's almost always with me but sometimes hard to find. Look for him carefully.

KATHARINE: I see him! I see the rat!

GANESHA: This demonstrates the concept—so important to me!—that opposites—an elephant and a mouse—can live together happily. That love of good food (I am always eating) and profound spiritual knowledge can go together. That a fat, rotund person can still be a supreme connoisseur of dance and music. In fact, I prove that the world is full of opposites which exist peacefully side by side.

KATHARINE: You can stop right there. I'm sold. Do you come any smaller? I couldn't possibly lug you back to Connecticut like that.

GANESHA: Let me check for you.

(*Lights fade on* GANESHA *as* MARGARET *and* MAN *appear again, still dancing.* KATHARINE *watches them.* MAN *whispers something in* MARGARET*'s ear. She throws her head back and laughs.*)

KATHARINE: May I cut in?

MARGARET: No.

MAN: I'm sorry.

(*They dance away from her.*)

MARGARET: Was that terrible of us?

MAN: Terribly! You're very beautiful.

MARGARET: Thank you.

MAN: For your years.

MARGARET: Did you have to say that?

MAN: Are you happy? (*He stops dancing.*)

MARGARET (*wanting to resume*): Yes. No. I don't know. Does it matter? Are you? Please, don't look at me like that.

(*He kisses her.*)

MAN: You should be happy.

MARGARET: I can't be.

MAN: I never knew what hit me. (*He snaps his fingers.*) Like that.

(*He goes.*)

(*Lights up on* GANESHA. *He approaches* KATHARINE *with a small carving of himself.*)

GANESHA: Is this small enough, excellent lady?

(*He hands it to* KATHARINE.)

> I come key-ring and necklace-pendant size, too, but when I get that small I only come in plastic and you lose all the detail.

KATHARINE: Excuse me, did you say "I"? "*I* only come in plastic"?

GANESHA: Oh, Lordy, no! That would be blasphemy.

KATHARINE: This one is perfect. What's it made of?

GANESHA: I believe that's amethyst, but let me check. Solar! My wife has all the answers. Solar!

KATHARINE: How much?

GANESHA: Fifty rupees?

KATHARINE: I'll take two. My friend, Mrs. Civil, is back in our hotel room writhing in agony. Her stomach. Montezuma's Revenge, they call it in Mexico. What do you call it here?

GANESHA: Just dysentery. We have no sense of humor when it comes to the bowels.

KATHARINE: Margaret would say, "That's something"!

GANESHA: You must not drink our water. Or eat our fruit. No matter how tempting.

KATHARINE: She didn't.

GANESHA: That's what you all say.

KATHARINE: But she didn't!

GANESHA: Solar!

(*He goes.*)

KATHARINE: I'm hoping this will cheer her up!

(*She looks down at the carving in her hand. So does* MARGARET.)

Isn't he darling? Maybe he'll help me get back that camera
I lost in Jodhpur. George is going to kill me.

MARGARET (*reading*): "I'm happy and I want people to be
happy, too." Thank you, Kitty.

KATHARINE: I'm just glad you're better. You're going to miss
India at this rate. The Towers of Silence were the highlight
of Bombay and you completely missed them.

MARGARET: I thought you couldn't see them.

KATHARINE: No, I said you just couldn't see the vultures actually
eating the flesh off the bones, if that's what you're talking
about. You have to be a Parsi. But you could stand outside
looking up at the towers and see the vultures swooping
down on the bodies on top. That was quite enough for this
cookie, thank you very much. Talk about feeling mortal.
That could have been me up there! One day it will be. When
I go, that's what I want done, Margaret. Just leave me out
on the pier at the Greenwich Yacht Club and let the seagulls
go to work.

(*The telephone begins to ring wanly again.*)

I'm not even going to answer it anymore. I'm glad you like
him. I thought you would.

(*The sounds of a train are heard; they will increase.*)

MARGARET: I just want to know why he has a head for an
elephant?

KATHARINE: What?

MARGARET: I mean, why he has an elephant's head?

KATHARINE: What? I can't hear you!

(*Transition as sounds of train level out to:*)

SCENE TWO

The Palace on Wheels, India's legendary luxury train. Teatime.
MARGARET, KATHARINE, *and the* MAN. *The* MAN *is an* AU-
THORITY. *He is examining a figure of Ganesha.*

MARGARET: I wish they kept these windows cleaner. How are
we supposed to see anything! How's your side?

KATHARINE (*miserably*): The same.

MARGARET: I told you to take Pepto-Bismol.

MAN (*returning the Ganesha*): It's soapstone.

KATHARINE: They said it was amethyst.

MAN: I'm surprised he didn't tell you it was marble. That's their
usual ploy, God love 'em! No, it's soapstone. I'm afraid
they saw you coming, Mrs. Brynne.

MARGARET: That's what I told her. Maybe she'll listen to you.

KATHARINE: I don't care what he's made of. I love him.

MARGARET: Kitty's become besotted with this Ganesh/Ganesha
person.

KATHARINE: He's not a person. He's a god. And I'm not besotted
with him.

MARGARET: I'm just hoping someone will tell us how he got his
elephant's head.

MAN: It's a dreadful story. I don't think Mrs. Brynne wants to
hear it on that stomach of hers.

KATHARINE: I'm fine.

MAN: Let's get some tea first.

(*He rings.*)

So you two ladies have fallen under the spell of Ganesha, too? Most travelers to India do. My first trip I couldn't get enough of him. I started developing this lump in the middle of my forehead. A sort of psychosomatic trunk.

KATHARINE: He's kidding, Margaret.

MARGARET: I know that. I knew that.

KATHARINE: I'm not besotted. I'm curious. I don't think Mrs. Civil is enjoying India.

MARGARET: That's not true.

KATHARINE: I adore it, of course.

MAN: Hindu mythology is so violent. It gives me the creeps. I'll settle for a hammer and nails, your basic wooden cross, and a nice Jewish boy any day of the week. I hope I haven't offended anyone.

KATHARINE: Just about everyone.

MAN: You two are a trip. I'm so glad I ran into you.

KATHARINE: Why, thank you, kind sir! You should see me when my guts don't feel like someone has got their hands in there and is tying them in knots.

MARGARET: She'd be dancing on the table.

MAN (*to* KATHARINE): You know, you remind me of someone: my mother.

KATHARINE: Ow! Such cramps. Out of the blue. Just when you think they've—! Ow! Ow! Ow!

MARGARET: I told her: don't eat that papaya.

KATHARINE: It wasn't a papaya! I thought peeling it would make it safe.

(GANESHA *appears. He carries a tray.*)

MAN: Tea for three, please. Understand? Tea for three.

KATHARINE (as GANESHA *hurries off*): *Ladesh.*

MARGARET (*anticipating what* KATHARINE *will say*): "That's Hindi for 'thank you.'"

KATHARINE (*to* MAN): That's Hindi for "thank you."

MARGARET: What did I tell you?

MAN: My wife would get such a kick out of you two!

KATHARINE: I can't believe she just flew home without you.

MAN: She couldn't take India. A lot of people can't. Too much poverty, too much disease.

KATHARINE: Too much everything. The colors, the smells, the sounds. My head is whirling, when my stomach isn't heaving.

MARGARET: Our husbands wouldn't even consider coming with us. "No way, Jose" was how Alan put it.

MAN: Actually, we had an incident in Benares. Are you going there?

KATHARINE: Absolutely. Benares is one of the reasons I most wanted to come to India.

MARGARET: You never told me that.

KATHARINE: What happened?

MAN: I don't want to upset you or anything, and I'm sure this won't happen to you, but we were down at the ghats where they burn the bodies. I've always been terrified of death and I thought maybe just looking at it would help. Hundreds of dead bodies being burned like so many logs. Who knew? Maybe it *would* help, and besides, people like us, we don't go to Benares without seeing the burning ghats, am I right?

KATHARINE: Go on.

MAN: They were burning the body of an old woman. I wish I could say I thought it was beautiful or spiritual, but I thought it was horrible and it scared the shit out of me. Kelly was holding my hand so tight I thought she would puncture my flesh with her nails. "I hate this, you bastard," she kept saying. Suddenly, someone called out behind us. A harsh, ugly sound. We turned and this wretched figure in rags on the ground was pointing at us and yelling. We started to run but Kelly tripped, I lost my grip on her, and she fell on top of him. When their bodies hit, he somehow seemed to throw his arms around her, hug her almost, and they rolled over and over in the mud. I couldn't pull them apart. Kelly was screaming but he wouldn't let go. Finally, it seemed like forever, two policemen appeared and they pulled him off her and apologized and then hit the old man with their truncheons and escorted us back to our hotel.

MARGARET (*to* KATHARINE): You're not going to the burning ghats!

MAN: I don't know if he was a leper, Kelly says he was, but she did say, "I will never, ever be clean again. I know it." She took shower after shower after shower but nothing would convince her that she was rid of him: his smell, his dirt, his essence, I suppose. I haven't heard from her since she got back to Boston. Poor baby. Let's hope.

KATHARINE: You didn't think of going back with her?

MAN: We don't have that sort of marriage. No children and we're very independent.

KATHARINE: But still . . .

MAN: I don't expect other people to understand. Besides, being in India is rather a solo project anyway. It's finally just you and it. India, ten; Kelly, nothing.

(GANESHA *has returned with the tea.*)

Thank you. (*To* KATHARINE:) What was that word?

KATHARINE: *Ladesh.*

MAN: *Ladesh.*

(*The compartment suddenly goes dark. The train has entered a tunnel.*)

MARGARET: What happened?!

KATHARINE: It's just a tunnel.

MAN: A long one, ladies. You haven't read your guide books. The Chittaurgarh Pass. The longest tunnel in India. Nearly forty-two kilometers.

MARGARET: What is that in miles?

MAN: I don't know. Thirty-five miles or so.

KATHARINE: If this were a movie, one of us would have a dagger in his back when he came out of it!

MAN: Or been kissed or pinched or both.

KATHARINE: You have a romantic imagination.

MAN: And you have a morbid one!

KATHARINE: You were going to tell us how Ganesh got his elephant's head.

MAN: All right, but I warned you.

MARGARET: Are we really going to be in a dark tunnel for the next hour?

KATHARINE: We're fine, Margaret. Nothing's going to happen.

MARGARET: Palace on Wheels! Dungeon on Wheels is more like it.

KATHARINE: Ignore her. Go ahead.

MARGARET: There was a dead spider in my bed last night.

MAN: Where was I?

MARGARET: I won't even go into the food!

MAN: Oh, Ganesha's head!

MARGARET: Oh! That wasn't funny.

KATHARINE: What?

MARGARET: Whoever did that, I didn't appreciate it.

(GANESHA *strikes a match and lights a kerosene lamp for them.*)

MAN: *Ladesh. Ladesh.*

KATHARINE: What's the matter, Margaret?

MARGARET: Someone . . . I distinctly felt a hand. . . .

KATHARINE: What?

MARGARET: On my breast. Someone . . . touched it. . . .

KATHARINE: Margaret.

MARGARET: I'm sure of it.

KATHARINE: Was it a friendly hand?

MARGARET: I'm serious.

KATHARINE: I'm sure whatever it was—if it was anything—just felt like a hand.

MARGARET: I guess I still know what a hand on my breasts feels like, Katharine, even if you don't remember.

KATHARINE: What is that supposed to mean?

MARGARET: I think you know.

GANESHA: Is there something wrong? The lady seems agitated.

MARGARET: What's he saying?

GANESHA: The tea was not good? I shall bring more candles?

MARGARET: I didn't accuse him. I don't know what he's babbling about.

(GANESHA *is in a dither.*)

KATHARINE: Well, who else were you accusing?

MAN: I can assure you, Mrs. Civil, grabbing women's breasts in dark railway tunnels is not my thing.

MARGARET: I didn't say it was.

MAN: And I doubt it was our porter. He's gay as a goose, can't you tell?

GANESHA (*with a napkin*): Crumbs on the lady! Here, let me—!

(*He moves to brush off her chest with his serving napkin.* MARGARET *pushes him away.*)

MARGARET: No!

GANESHA: I have done something wrong? I have given offense?

MAN: Fine! Everything is fine!

MARGARET: Everything is not fine.

KATHARINE: Now who's the Ugly American!

MARGARET: This isn't about that, Kitty.

KATHARINE: And I won't forget that remark about George.

MARGARET: What remark?

KATHARINE: He touches me just fine! What would you know about it?

MAN: Ladies, please!

GANESHA: The lady is frightened of the tunnel? Tell the lady there is nothing to fear. See? I laugh at the tunnel. Ha ha ha!

KATHARINE: What is he doing?

GANESHA: Ha ha ha!

MAN: Go! Go back to where you came from!

GANESHA: Ganesha loves you. Ganesha will protect you.

KATHARINE: Wait! He said something about Ganesha. Did you say Ganesha?

GANESHA (*joyfully*): Ganesha, yes, Ganesha!

KATHARINE: There, hear that? He said "Ganesha."

MARGARET: I suppose Ganesha fondled my breast!

GANESHA: Ganesha! Ganesha!

KATHARINE: Now it's "fondled." First it was just "touched." Next we'll be having the Malabar Caves incident.

GANESHA (*fearfully*): Malabar! No, no! No, Malabar!

KATHARINE: I'm not accusing you!

GANESHA: No, Malabar! Bad, Malabar! You wrong! No, Malabar! I am going to my supervisor and tell him the truth before you ladies lie and have Anant made redundant. Malabar, no!

(*He goes.*)

KATHARINE: What did I say? Rather, what did he think I said?

MAN: The one porter in all Rajasthan who's read *Passage to India*.

MARGARET: I'm glad you find this so amusing.

KATHARINE: No one finds it amusing, Margaret, but we can't go around accusing people because we feel superior to them.

MARGARET: I don't feel superior to that person.

KATHARINE: Yes, you do. So do I. And by our standards, we are. That's the terrible thing.

MARGARET: Spare us this, Kitty.

MAN: If you ladies will excuse me, but I've already done this part with Kelly.

KATHARINE: We're sorry.

MAN: I saw a three-month-old copy of the *Village Voice* with a review of Bob Dylan at the Garden in the library. Or what Indian Rail calls the library. Bob Dylan! God, we're all getting so old.

(*He goes.*)

MARGARET: No, he doesn't remind me of Walter, either.

KATHARINE: I wasn't going to say that.

MARGARET: There is evil in the world, Katharine.

KATHARINE: I know that.

MARGARET: And I was just subjected to some of it.

KATHARINE: So was my son.

MARGARET: Do you want to cut the trip short?

KATHARINE: No. Do you?

MARGARET: No.

(*Long pause. The sound of the train gets louder and louder.*)

    I'm sorry.

KATHARINE: It's all right. So am I. So am I.

(*Suddenly the train comes out of the tunnel and the light will seem very bright.*)

I thought he said we'd be in there for an hour.

MARGARET: That type thinks they know everything.

KATHARINE: I thought you liked him.

MARGARET: I did, for fifteen minutes. Look, there's some nice scenery coming up.

(*They look out the window on different sides of the compartment.*)

I like everyone for fifteen minutes.

KATHARINE: Thank you.

MARGARET: Don't be ridiculous. You're my oldest friend.

KATHARINE: We hardly know each other.

MARGARET: That's not true. We know each other. We love each other. We just don't especially like each other. I've got water buffaloes on my side. What do you have?

KATHARINE: Camels.

MARGARET: I would imagine people had this same view thousands of years ago, before electricity, before television and atomic bombs, before we all got so neurotic. You were born, you grew up, you worked in a field like those, you got married, you had children, you got old, you died, and with a little luck, somebody remembered you kindly for at least one generation.

KATHARINE: I don't feel like I'm in India. I see sky and hills and horizons and trees. What makes it India and not Danbury? We travel, but we don't go anywhere. I'm stuck right here. The earth spins but I don't.

(GANESHA *appears in the compartment.*)

GANESHA: Excuse me, ladies, I understand there was some disturbance here? Some confusion?

MARGARET: No, nothing, we're fine. We're both fine.

KATHARINE: Yes, thank you.

GANESHA: But I was told—

MARGARET: Really, it's quite forgotten. When are we getting to Jaipur?

GANESHA: At exactly 23:30. In time for the fireworks and the great Hali Festival.

KATHARINE: I have a feeling we won't be three for dinner this evening.

GANESHA: Ah, yes, the gentleman already explained that. Goodbye then.

(*He goes.*)

MARGARET: I wish I could be a better friend to you, Kitty, and vice versa. I don't know what stops me.

KATHARINE: Thank you for not making an issue about your breast.

MARGARET: It's that good Yankee breeding, don't you know. It's all in the genes and we all have these marvelous cheekbones and talk like Katharine Hepburn. We're both the same age and we're from the same background—

KATHARINE: Or so you thought!

MARGARET: Our husbands make approximately the same living. We're both mothers.

KATHARINE: You never lost a child.

MARGARET: Well, that's true.

KATHARINE: Nothing compares to losing a child. No, nothing compares to losing that particular child. Why couldn't it have been his brother or Nan or one of her kids or George even? Do you think God will strike me dead for saying something like that?

MARGARET: Of course not.

KATHARINE: I think maybe he should. Every time the phone rang I dreaded it being him and him saying, "Mom, I've got it. I've got AIDS."

MARGARET: You want to talk about it?

KATHARINE: What is there to say? Who the hell are you to tell me there's evil in the world? You think some little brown man touched your tit in a tunnel. I'm surprised the earth didn't spin off its axis! I know what one, two, three, four, five, six—count 'em: six!—African-Americans did to my son at two-thirty in the morning at the corner of Barrow and Greenwich. They get off (Walter was a faggot, after all!) and I don't even get to say "nigger"! I know there's evil. I'm not so sure there's any justice.

MARGARET: I wish I could comfort you.

KATHARINE: I wish you could, too. Now I've got the water buffaloes.

MARGARET: May I put my arm around you?

KATHARINE: I'd rather you wouldn't.

(MARGARET *puts her arm around her.*)

MARGARET: You don't have to say anything. Sshh! Sshh! I'm not going to say anything.

KATHARINE: Thank you for that, at least.

MARGARET: You're not alone, Kitty. I'm here. Another person, another woman, is here. Right here. Breathing the same air.

Riding the same train. Looking out the window at the same timeless landscape. You are not alone. Even in your agony.

KATHARINE: Thank you.

MARGARET: I love you. I love you very much. Offamof.

KATHARINE: What?

MARGARET: Offamof.

KATHARINE: Oh, yeah—Offamof!

(*Lights up on* GANESHA. *He comes down to us as the sounds of the train come up and the lights dim on* MARGARET *and* KATHARINE.)

GANESHA: And so it happened that while Margaret Civil and Katharine Brynne stared with heavy, sad, sad eyes at what Mr. Ray of India Rail injudiciously called the most beautiful scenery in India, some 8,345 miles away, at 11:20 p.m. their time, George Brynne, Katharine Brynne's husband, Caucasian male, aged sixty-two, lost control of his car on a patch of something called glare ice on his way home from a movie Katharine had refused to see because of its purported violence (she was right! an appalling motion picture it was, too!), went into a skid and slammed into a three-hundred-year-old oak tree. He died instantly. Mrs. Brynne will not learn of her loss until she gets home. Since her children cannot reach her by phone (the ladies are off their itinerary and frequently without reservations; in Khajuraho they slept on two cots in the garden of a sympathetic postmaster), her children decide it is better to meet her at the airport when she and Mrs. Civil return.

(*Lights are coming up on* MARGARET *and* KATHARINE. *The sounds of the train have faded. We hear the periodic ringing of a temple bell.*)

MARGARET: I can't believe you've actually lost your guidebook, Kitty.

KATHARINE: Sooner or later I lose everything.

MARGARET: How are you going to know what you're looking at?

KATHARINE: I am putting myself completely in the hands of our guide, Mr. Kamlesh Tandu of Jodhpur.

GANESHA (*to us*): I think Mrs. Brynne has a slight "thing" for me, I believe you call them. It's very curious but not uncommon. In her own country she wouldn't give me the time of day.

MARGARET: Well, don't come running to me when we leave Mr. Tandu in Jaisalmer and you want to know what something is. I'm not going to tell you.

KATHARINE: As Rudyard Kipling said, "Oh, bugger off, Margaret!"

MARGARET: I'm sure Rudyard Kipling never said "Bugger off, Margaret." Somerset Maugham maybe.

GANESHA (*stepping forward*): Welcome to my humble village, lovely ladies. No television, no electricity. Puppet shows and traveling players are our windows on the world. It's lovely.

KATHARINE: You said you had a treat for us, Mr. Tandu.

GANESHA: No, for you, Mrs. Brynne. That is, if you don't mind, Mrs. Civil.

MARGARET: Not in the least.

KATHARINE: Why just for me?

GANESHA: Why not? (*He claps his hands.*) Puppets, please!

SCENE THREE

A village square. Dusk. A puppet show is in progress. The MAN *is a* PUPPETEER. *There are three camp stools for* MARGARET, KATHARINE, *and* GANESHA.

GANESHA: Once again, lovely ladies, "How Lovely Lord Ganesha Got His Lovely Elephant's Head." Puppets, please.

(*He has handed* KATHARINE *a small book.*)

KATHARINE: What's this?

GANESHA: Your part. In India we participate in theatre. We don't sit back, arms folded, and say "Show me."

(MARGARET *has been sitting exactly like that.*)

MARGARET: I'm sorry.

KATHARINE: "Still in a fury that his wife would not see him, Shiva sent his forces to kill the boy who barred his way."

GANESHA: Very good!

KATHARINE: "But Parvati created two shaktis to defend her son against her husband, Kali and Durga."

MAN (*showing the puppets*): Kali and Durga!

MARGARET: What's a shakti, Mr. Tandu?

GANESHA: I believe you call them she-devils, Mrs. Civil.

KATHARINE: No, we say bitches. Don't interrupt, Margaret. This is my big moment. "To his amazement, Shiva's forces were completely routed by the valiant youth. He knew what he must do."

MAN: "I will have to kill the boy with my own hands. Let it never be said that a man was subservient to his wife!"

MARGARET: That sounds familiar.

KATHARINE: "Shiva charged the boy with his silver-shining tri-
dent but the boy swung his iron club and sent him sprawl-
ing." Good for the boy!

MAN: "That should teach you a lesson, old man, Pop."

(KATHARINE *looks up from the book.*)

KATHARINE: What?

MAN (*to* KATHARINE): "Mother, see how I serve you."

(*From this point,* KATHARINE *will not be able to take her eyes
off the puppets and the* MAN. *She will let the playbook lie open
in her lap.*)

GANESHA: And the boy laughed. Oh, how he laughed!

MAN: Ha ha ha! Ha ha ha!

MARGARET: Ha ha ha! Ha ha ha! This is charming.

GANESHA: And while the boy laughed, Shiva came up from behind him and with one swift stroke of his sword, cut off
Walter's head.

MAN: Whoosh. Ung.

GANESHA: He could hear the sound against the side of his head.

MAN: Whoosh. Ung.

GANESHA: Shiva had landed a good one. You're not looking,
Mrs. Brynne.

MAN: I stayed on my feet a remarkably long time, Mama. I was
sort of proud of me.

KATHARINE (*looking back to the book*): Where does it say that?

MAN: "Mother, see how I serve you."

KATHARINE: He's not following the script.

GANESHA: And down he fell.

KATHARINE: Why me, Mr. Tandu?

GANESHA: Again, why not you, Mrs. Brynne? As the boy lay dying, Shiva realized what he had done.

KATHARINE: Shiva, not I! (*She abruptly stands up.*)

MARGARET: Where are you going?

GANESHA: You must hear the story to its end, Mrs. Brynne.

KATHARINE: I know how it ends. In a New York hospital. Twenty minutes before I got there.

GANESHA: No, it ends in reconciliation, renewal, and rebirth.

KATHARINE: Tell it to Mrs. Civil.

(*She hands the playbook to* MARGARET *and goes.*)

MARGARET: I think your story upset Mrs. Brynne.

GANESHA: Perhaps she needed upsetting, Mrs. Civil. May we continue? It is very bad form to abandon Lord Ganesha in midstream. Shiva went to his wife and begged forgiveness for what he had done.

MAN: "O, great goddess, wife and mother, forgive me."

GANESHA: Parvati faced him with great dignity. That's you, Mrs. Civil.

MARGARET: "I will forgive. But my son must regain his life, and he must have an honorable status among you."

GANESHA: Lord Shiva responded with great humility.

MAN: "Your will shall be done. Vishnu, go north. Bring the head of the first creature that crosses your path. Fit that head to the boy's body and it will come to life."

MARGARET: And the first creature they saw was an elephant! With a single tusk!

GANESHA: Vishnu threw his golden discus and killed him.

MARGARET: And they cut off his head and fitted it to the body of her little boy.

GANESHA: The boy sat up.

MARGARET: He was reborn.

MAN: Then Shiva placed his hand on the boy's head and pronounced these solemn and healing words.

GANESHA: "Even as a mere boy you showed great valor. You shall be Ganesha, the presiding officer of all my ganas. You shall be worthy of worship forever."

MAN: Mighty is the Lord Shiva, great is his compassion.

GANESHA: Here ends the story of how Lord Ganesha got his lovely head.

MARGARET: Thank you.

GANESHA: There are many others, Mrs. Civil, if the ladies are so inclined.

MARGARET: I don't think so. I'm worried about my friend.

GANESHA: I said something wrong perhaps?

MARGARET: It almost seemed deliberate.

GANESHA: It's only a legend. You Christians take everything so literally.

MARGARET: She had a son who . . .

GANESHA: Whose head was cut off? My, my, my! This New York City of yours must be a fearful place.

MARGARET: Don't be ridiculous. His head wasn't cut off. He was murdered.

MAN: I heard of a man who went there and they ate his toes they were so hungry.

MARGARET: Don't believe such stories. I assure you, it hasn't come to that.

MAN (*to* GANESHA, *unconvinced*): They sold his eyeballs for drug money.

MARGARET: You have a horrible imagination.

MAN: Thanking you very much.

MARGARET: Work on your English. It wasn't a compliment.

(*She starts walking in the opposite direction to the one* KATHARINE *took.*)

MARGARET: Katharine! Kitty!

GANESHA: Tonight they ride elephants to a banquet in a maharajah's palace and dine by torchlight. Oh, lordy, look at me! I have to dress. *Sayonara. Ciao.*

(*Lights fade on* MAN *and* GANESHA *while* MARGARET *and* KATHARINE *walk. Again, a turntable would be useful.*)

MARGARET: Kitty! Kitty!

KATHARINE: God, leave me alone, woman. All of you. No more guides or puppets. No more India. I want to go home and forget I ever came here. I'm sick of your mythology. It's as false as ours. My son was not reborn. He died twenty minutes before I got to the hospital. His murderers never asked my forgiveness. You had it easy, Parvati. No honor has ever been made to me. I have my anger and nothing more. No love. No love at all.

MARGARET: Katherine! Kitty! Now where is she gone to? She'd lose herself and not just the train tickets if I didn't keep an eye on her. I'm ashamed to admit it, but I never realized how dependent we are on the men. She won't admit that, but it's true. This may be the last time I go anywhere with anyone. I'm not a fellow traveler. I almost told her about Gabriel. It would have been such a tiny leap across that void between two people. "I lost a son too, Kitty." Six little words and I couldn't do it. "I lost a son too, Kitty." Kitty!

(KATHARINE *has started walking with* GANESHA.)

KATHARINE: How old are you? Do you speak any English? Seven years old? Eight? How old are you?

(MARGARET *has started walking with the* MAN. *He is a* FOREIGN TOURIST.)

MARGARET: Dutch? We've been to Holland. Twice. You have wonderful museums there. The Rembrandt Museum, one of my favorites.

MAN: Yes, Rembrandt.

MARGARET: My favorite painting is by Rembrandt, only it's in London at the National Gallery.

MAN: London, yes?

KATHARINE: You have the dearest face! Oh God, I wish I knew your name. When I get back to America I would send you the biggest box of anything you wanted.

GANESHA: Are you from America? How old are you? Are you rich? Is there really a Rocky? Who is your leader there now?

KATHARINE: Slow down, slow down! I don't understand a word you're saying. I do not speak Hindi.

GANESHA: I like you.

KATHARINE: Where are we going? I'm letting you take me.

MARGARET: It's called *Woman Bathing*.

MAN: Yes?

MARGARET: Well, in English it's called *Woman Bathing*. I don't know what it's called in Dutch. Do you know it?

MAN: Yes, *Woman Bathing*?

MARGARET: It's just a woman wading in a river. She has her shift pulled up to her thighs. She's looking at herself in the reflection of the water. She's very pensive but very powerful, too. It's a dark painting, most Rembrandt is, but there's something about it. Her isolation. Her independence. Her strength. I'm terrible talking about art. Are you good at it?

MAN: Yes?

(*A bolt of blue fabric is rolled across the white floor of the stage. It is a river.* KATHARINE *and* MARGARET *will find themselves on different sides of it.*)

MARGARET: Oh, look, there's a river here. Can we sit and bathe our feet?

MAN: Very nice.

(*They sit.*)

KATHARINE: So this is where you were leading me? What's this river called?

MARGARET: Kitty, hello! Kitty! There's my friend on the other side of the river.

KATHARINE: Hello! That's Mrs. Civil. She is my friend.

MARGARET: She can't hear us. Who's your little friend?

KATHARINE: Behave yourself, you two! What is she doing?

(MARGARET *has started wading in the river.*)

MARGARET: *Woman Bathing* by Rembrandt!

MAN: *Woman Bathing*, ah, yes! Ha ha ha.

KATHARINE: You're a happy little person, aren't you? What's your secret? Everyone in India seems so content. I'm sure that's not true, but you seem to possess some inner calm or confidence that we don't. I bet if I put even one finger on your belly you'll fall over giggling like a little doughboy!

(*She touches* GANESHA *in the stomach and he falls over giggling. She will continue to tickle him awhile. He is enjoying himself enormously.*)

MARGARET: Every time I go to London I visit it. But the last time I looked at it something strange and rather awful happened. Two museum guards were talking as if I weren't there. One was a man, more or less my age, talking to a much younger woman, who I assume was Indian or from Pakistan. You know what he said to her? Right in front of me, as if I were invisible! "No one wants me anymore. I've had my day. It's gone now." I wish people wouldn't say such deeply personal things in public. It stayed with me our entire trip. It almost ruined my Rembrandt. This was five or six years ago. It just came back to me.

MAN: London. Father's sister, London.

MARGARET: "No one wants me anymore. I've had my day. It's gone now." Isn't that a terrible thing to say with a total stranger listening?

KATHARINE: They're going back.

(*She waves and calls across to* MARGARET *and* MAN.)

I'll see you in the room.

MARGARET (*waving and calling*): Five o'clock! Drinks with the manager!

(MARGARET *and* MAN *withdraw.*)

(*Light change suggests the passage of time.*)

(GANESHA*'s head is lying in* KATHARINE*'s lap.*)

KATHARINE: My little brown bambino. My nutmeg Gesu. What color is your skin? Coffee? That's not right either. What color is mine? Not white. Where do words come from? What do they mean?

GANESHA: Walter.

KATHARINE: What? I thought you said "Walter."

GANESHA: Walter.

KATHARINE: You did! You did say "Walter"!

GANESHA: Walter.

KATHARINE: Walter must be a word in Hindi then! Yes? Tell me, what does it mean, "Walter"?

GANESHA (*laughing merrily*): Walter! Walter!

(*He suddenly throws his arms around her and holds her tight.*)

KATHARINE: Does it mean "laughter"? It means something joyful! Something good! It must! Walter! Walter!

(SHE *puts her hands to her mouth and calls across the lake.*)

Walter! Walter!

(GANESHA *imitates her.*)

GANESHA: Walter! Walter!

(*There is an echo.*)

ECHO: Walter! Walter!

(*There is a silence as the echo dies away.*)

KATHARINE: It's gone.

GANESHA: Why have you stopped smiling?

(*She kisses him fiercely.*)

KATHARINE: Stay this way forever. When you grow up, I won't like you. I will hate you and fear you because of the color of your skin—just as I hated and feared my son because he loved men. I won't tell you this to your face but you will know it, just as he did, and it will sicken and diminish us both.

GANESHA: Why are you looking at me so intently? What do you want to see?

KATHARINE: I came here to heal, but I can't forgive myself. Maybe if I shout out the names of my fear and hatred of you across this holy river they will vanish, too, just as Walter did. Faggot. Queer. The words keep sticking.

GANESHA (*trying to imitate her, like before*): Faggot? Queer?

KATHARINE: A small boy says it better than you.

GANESHA: Faggot? Queer?

KATHARINE: Again.

GANESHA (*happily, for her approval*): Faggot! Queer!

KATHARINE: Again!

GANESHA (*bigger*): Faggot! Queer!

KATHARINE: Louder!

GANESHA: Faggot! Faggot! Queer! Queer!

KATHARINE: No, with hatred! Like they did: Fag! Queer! Cocksucker! Dead-from-AIDS queer meat!

GANESHA: Oh dear, oh dear!

KATHARINE: FAGGOT! FAGGOT! QUEER! QUEER! NIGGER!

(KATHARINE *begins to break down. In the silence, we hear only her sobs.*)

ECHO: Faggot, faggot! Queer, queer! Walter! Walter!

KATHARINE: Walter. Forgive me.

(GANESHA *cradles* KATHARINE *at the bank of the river.*)

(MAN *has appeared as* WALTER. *He waves to* KATHARINE, *blows her a kiss, and disappears.*)

GANESHA: Foolish woman. You were holding a god in your arms.

(*Lights change.* KATHARINE *stays where she is.* GANESHA *picks up a long pole. He is a* BOATMAN.)

(*Sounds of water lapping.*)

MARGARET: We're coming! We're coming.

(MARGARET *enters, hair covered by a scarf. The* MAN *is with her. He is a* GUIDE.)

SCENE FOUR

On the Ganges River in Varanasi. MARGARET, KATHARINE, *and* MAN *sit in a small skiff, piloted by* GANESHA. *It is early morning and very misty.*

MARGARET (*holding a pair of binoculars*): Look what you left in the room! We wouldn't have seen a thing. Thank God I went back for a scarf.
　　　　Is someone going to give me a hand?

(GANESHA *puts his hand out to her as she steps aboard the skiff. It threatens to capsize.*)

　　　　Oh my God! Is this safe? Are we all going to drown in the Ganges?

MAN: Not if you sit down, Mrs. Civil!

MARGARET: I can't sit down until it stops rocking.

GANESHA: She's going to make us capsize.

MAN: Grab the sides and sit!

(MARGARET *steadies herself and sits.* GANESHA *will help* MAN *aboard the skiff and then guide it out into the river.*)

MARGARET: This is madness. I'm never going to see Pumpkin Fields Lane again. I hate you for doing this. I hate myself for coming.

MAN (*to* GANESHA): Thank you.

MARGARET (*to* GANESHA): Oh, yes, thank you! (*Then:*) Who would think to bring Dramamine to India? Dramamine is for when we take the *QE2*. Where's your scarf? Mr. Tennyson warned us about this damp morning air. You just got over dysentery. Next stop, pneumonia. Then on to God knows what!

KATHARINE: Margaret, please, sshh!

MARGARET: You're right, I'm sorry. I'll practice what they taught us at the yoga institute in Delhi. Om! It's not working. Don't mind me, everyone. They're not. That's what's so pathetic!

MAN: Benares, now called Varanasi, the "eternal city," is one of the most important pilgrimage sites in India and also a major tourist attraction.

MARGARET: Oh my God, look at that: a dead rat floating by.

MAN: For the pious Hindu, the city has always had a special meaning. Besides being a pilgrimage center, it is considered especially auspicious to die here, insuring an instant routing to heaven.

MARGARET: Oh my God, what's that?

GANESHA: Cow!

MARGARET: What's he saying?

GANESHA: Cow!

MARGARET: It looks like a cow.

MAN: I think it is.

GANESHA: Cow!

MARGARET: What's the Hindi word for "cow"?

MAN: I don't know.

MARGARET: I'm going to be sick.

KATHARINE: Tell us about the ghats, Mr. Tennyson.

MAN: Ghats are the steps which lead down to the river, from which pilgrims make their sin-cleansing dip in the Ganges. Dawn is the best time to visit them.

MARGARET: Oh my God, Kitty, look! It's a body.

KATHARINE: I see it, Margaret.

MAN: The pilgrims will be there for their early morning dip, the city will just be coming to life, the light is magical.

MARGARET: We're going to bump right into it!

(*We hear the thud of the body against the skiff.*)

MAN: There are one hundred ghats in all, of which—

KATHARINE: Tell us about the burning ghats.

MAN: There are two principal ones, the Marnikarnika ghat and the Charanpaduka ghat. There, you can just see the fires. This is where bodies are cremated after making the final journey to the holy Ganges—the men swathed in white cloth, the women in red—and carried on a bamboo stretcher—or even the roof of a taxi.

GANESHA: Baby!

MARGARET: Oh my God, don't look, Kitty. It's a child.

GANESHA: Baby!

KATHARINE: Can you tell what sex it is?

MAN: Keep going, keep going!

GANESHA: Baby!

MARGARET: We're going to hit again!

(*Again we hear the sound of the body hitting against the side of the skiff.*)

   Oh, that sound!

(GANESHA *takes the skiff pole and pokes at the body.*)

GANESHA: Boy baby!

KATHARINE: It's a little boy.

MARGARET: How can you look even?!

MAN: Perhaps we should go back. Mrs. Civil doesn't seem able to handle this.

MARGARET: You're right, she's not. Please, Kitty, I've had enough.

MAN (*to* GANESHA): Back! Take us back!

(GANESHA *takes the pole from the body and resumes navigating the skiff. In so doing, he splashes some water on* MARGARET.)

MARGARET: Oh! Be careful! (*She brushes at the water on her clothes.*) He was poking that body with his pole! I feel slimy now.

KATHARINE: What brought you here, Mr. Tennyson?

MAN: It's Norman, please! I was looking for something I couldn't find in Wilkes-Barre, Pennsylvania. I forget what it was now, but for a couple of minutes, back there in my youth, I thought I'd found it. Maybe it was just extra-good grass.

(*The sound of another body against the skiff.*)

MARGARET: Please, can we get home?

KATHARINE: I thought I would be more appalled by all this.

MAN: Thought or hoped? Some people come to Varanasi to find their hearts have completely hardened. It's a terrible realization.

MARGARET: What are we supposed to do? I can't accept all this. My heart and mind would break if I did. And yet I must. I know it.

KATHARINE: Everything in and on this river seems inevitable and right. Something dead, floating there.

MARGARET: It's a dog.

KATHARINE: That old woman with the sagging breasts bathing herself, oblivious to us.

MARGARET: She's lovely.

KATHARINE: Even us in our Burberry raincoats. We all have a place here. Nothing is right, nothing is wrong. Allow. Accept. Be.

MARGARET: Yes.

(GANESHA *brings the skiff to shore.* MAN *leaps off and helps the others to disembark.*)

MAN: Home again. I think you'll find the shopping here a little more to your liking. Varanasi is famous all over India for its silk brocade.

KATHARINE: I'm still looking for a figure of Ganesh.

MARGARET: You've already bought almost a dozen.

KATHARINE: I'm looking for a perfect Ganesh.

MAN: Is there such a thing?

KATHARINE: I'm sure of it.

MAN: Let's get a move on, ladies. We have Sarnath before lunch.

MARGARET: What's in Sarnath?

MAN: Buddha!

(*They walk away from* GANESHA, *who looks after them, brings his hands together, and bows.*)

GANESHA: You're welcome. You're welcome. You're welcome.

(*He has Margaret's binoculars, Katharine's first Ganesh figure, and the Man's Marlboros.*)

(*Lights are changing.*)

SCENE FIVE

A hotel room. There are louvered doors leading to a balcony fronting on a street.

KATHARINE: May I?

(MARGARET *stands with her back to us. She holds her blouse open to* KATHARINE, *who is sitting in front of her.*)

(*A dog is barking off. It stops.*)

(*In the silence:*)

    Oh!

(MARGARET *closes her blouse and begins to button it.*)

MARGARET: I don't know what annoys me more about this country: the heat, the music, or the barking dogs.

KATHARINE: How long have you known?

MARGARET: I wasn't sure until that first night in Bombay.

KATHARINE: We'll go back at once.

MARGARET: No, we've come this far, I want to see the Taj Mahal. It's just a few more days.

KATHARINE: But you promise you'll—?

MARGARET: Of course.

KATHARINE: Just as soon as we get back!

MARGARET: Absolutely.

KATHARINE: I'm so sorry, Margaret.

MARGARET: Well. And that's about as philosophical as I'm going to get. I don't want anyone else to know; unless I have to, of course.

KATHARINE: Of course not. Thank you for confiding in me. It means a good deal to me. More than you could know. I need a friend. That sounds ridiculous at my age. But you're going to tell Alan, of course?

MARGARET: I don't know. Not if I don't have to. It would give him one more reason to work late. He's had one reason for almost seven years. Her name is DeKennesey. She must be divorced. I know she's got two kids. I've seen them. She's only ten years younger than me. He's got her in one of those condos by the club.

KATHARINE: I had no idea.

MARGARET: We're not supposed to.

KATHARINE: I'm so sorry.

MARGARET: You've got to stop saying that. What happens to women? Who are we? What are we supposed to do? What are we supposed to be? Men still have all the marbles. All we have are our children, and sooner or later we lose them.

(*She goes to the louvered doors, opens them, and goes out.*)

(*Lights up on* MAN. *He is a leper, as hideous as the first one.*)

Your friend is back down there.

KATHARINE: You think I'm crazy, don't you?

MARGARET: Yes.

(KATHARINE *has joined* MARGARET *on the balcony looking down at the* MAN.)

KATHARINE: I couldn't do it. Yesterday, while you were resting, I went down to the lobby and ordered tea and just sat and stared at him out there. I felt so drawn to him, Margaret, yet so repulsed. I had to go out to him.

(*She moves out of the room and to the* MAN. MARGARET *stays on the balcony watching them.*)

MARGARET: I was up here. I wanted to call out to you but I didn't. I guess I wanted you to do it for the both of us.

KATHARINE: Why are you diseased and hideous? What can I do to change that?

MAN: Love me.

(*Lights up on* GANESHA, *again with his elephant's head.*)

GANESHA: "Love me," the man said, and smiled at the lovely American.

KATHARINE: Here, in the warmth and light of India, I want to hold you in my arms, as I could not hold my son while he lay dying on a dark city street.

MAN: Love me.

GANESHA: "Love me," the man said again, and smiled again.

KATHARINE: Now, in this moment when we are so close but so alone, I want to kiss you on the lips, as I could never kiss my son for fear of terrifying him with how much I loved him.

MAN: Love me.

GANESHA: "Love me," the man said again, but this time he did not smile.

KATHARINE: You frighten me. You disgust me.

MAN: Love me.

KATHARINE: I cannot do it.

GANESHA: And Mrs. Katharine Brynne reached into her purse and gave the man fifty rupees and one of her perfect Ganeshas. She did not sleep well that night. She worried about her soul. The man, however, had the finest meal of his entire, miserable life.

(KATHARINE *comes back to* MARGARET *on the balcony. Again they look down at the* MAN *just sitting there.*)

MARGARET: I couldn't do it, either.

KATHARINE: The whole trip was a failure then.

MARGARET: You're too hard on yourself. You can't save the world.

KATHARINE: I can't even save myself. Here.

(*She hands* MARGARET *another of her Ganeshas.*)

MARGARET: That's one of your favorites.

KATHARINE: There's plenty more where it came from. I've got more than a dozen of them now. I still haven't found the perfect one.

GANESHA: They're all perfect, Katharine.

(*With a gesture he reveals a dazzling array of all sorts of Ganeshas: stone, clay, ivory, etc.*)

KATHARINE: I know. I wish I could believe that. I can't. I just can't. (*To* MARGARET:) It's for good luck with—

MARGARET: You're a kind woman.

(*They just look at each other a moment. It would be hard to say who opens her arms to the other first. They embrace. They kiss.*)

KATHARINE: The Taj Mahal, then home.

MARGARET: The Taj Mahal!

(*Light change.*)

(*Blinding light. It should be hard to look at the stage.*)

(*Music.*)

SCENE SIX

The Taj Mahal. We see it through MARGARET *and* KATHARINE*'s eyes. They are transfixed.*

GANESHA: What does one say before such beauty? If one is wise, very, very little.

(*The* MAN *appears. He is another* AMERICAN TOURIST *reading from a guidebook.*)

MAN: "If there's a building which evokes a country—like the Eiffel Tower does for France, the Sydney Opera House for Australia—then it has to be the Taj Mahal for India."

MARGARET: Do you mind? We're trying to appreciate all this.

MAN: It's a free country.

KATHARINE: No, that's America. This is India.

(*He withdraws. The two women are in rapture.*)

MARGARET: I've stopped breathing.

KATHARINE: My heart is pounding.

MARGARET: This has been worth everything.

KATHARINE: It's the most beautiful thing I've ever seen.

MARGARET: I'm not going to cry. I refuse to cry.

KATHARINE: Go right ahead. I just may join you.

MARGARET: Do you think this is why we exist? To create this?

KATHARINE: I don't know. I don't think I can talk.

MARGARET: I think it's better maybe if we don't.

KATHARINE: I want you to see what I'm seeing. Look, over there!

MARGARET: I see it, I see it. And over there, Kitty, have you ever . . . ?

KATHARINE: We're in paradise. This is a dream. It isn't true.

MARGARET: But it is true. And we're here. And we will have this forever.

KATHARINE: Look!

MARGARET: Look!

(GANESHA *draws a filmy gauze drape across the stage. It is the first time the stage has been "closed" the entire evening.*)

GANESHA: Two days later, they were back in Connecticut, met at the airport by a solemn delegation of Alan Civil and various Brynnes bearing the mournful news of Katharine's husband, the glare ice and the oak tree. Vacations can end abruptly like this. Trips have a way of going on. Mrs. Civil and Mrs. Brynne's visit to India was of the second variety.

(*He pulls back the gauze curtain. To one side is a king-size bed.* KATHARINE *is undressing to get into it. On the other side, there are twin beds.* MARGARET *is getting ready to get into one of them. The* MAN *is already in his bed. He is* ALAN.)

MARGARET: What's this postcard? (*She picks up a postcard on the pillow.*)

MAN: It came yesterday. It was addressed to the two of you. What were you two doing over there? Picking up strange men? That was a joke, Margaret.

(MARGARET *sits on the edge of the bed and reads the card.*)

I'll never know if I did the right thing. But who knew where to find you? It's a big country. I said to their kids, go to the Taj Mahal, hang out, sooner or later, they'll turn up. Everybody thought I was kidding. I thought it was a good idea. Good night, Maggie, I'm glad you're home. I missed you.

(*He turns out the light.* MARGARET *picks up the phone and dials a number.*)

(KATHARINE *is sitting on the edge of her bed. She is humming/singing "Blow the Wind Southerly." The telephone rings.*)

KATHARINE: Yes?

MARGARET: Are you okay?

KATHARINE: Better than expected.

MARGARET: We got a postcard from Harry and Ben.

KATHARINE: I'm sorry, I don't—

MARGARET: Yes, you do! The two young men, next door, our first day in Bombay. They were both sick.

KATHARINE: I remember.

MARGARET: "Dear Girls, (all right, ladies!), welcome home! Hope you had a wonderful trip and didn't have to use that police whistle again. Did you see the Taj Mahal? Didn't you die just a little? Thanks for all your kindness. Harry is still in the hospital here but doing well. We're both hanging in there. What else are you gonna do? Love, Ben." Guess who the postcard's of? Your favorite, Ganesha. A perfect Ganesh. I'll bring it over tomorrow. Are you sure you're okay?

KATHARINE: I'm fine.

MARGARET: I love you.

KATHARINE: Thank you.

MARGARET: You're supposed to say "I love you, too."

KATHARINE: I love you, too, Margaret.

MARGARET: Good night, Kitty.

KATHARINE: Good night.

(*They hang up. They each are sitting on the edge of their beds.*)

(KATHARINE *begins to sing/hum "Blow the Wind Southerly."*)

(*The* MAN *has begun to snore.* MARGARET *looks at him, then at the postcard, and begins to sing/hum "Swing Low, Sweet Chariot."*)

(*At exactly the same time—i.e., simultaneously—the two women get into bed and under the covers.*)

(GANESHA *appears between them. He takes off his elephant's head. His face is gilded and he is revealed as a handsome man.*)

(*He bends over* MARGARET *and kisses her. She stops singing and sleeps. Then he bends over* KATHARINE *and kisses her. She, too, stops singing and sleeps.*)

(*The* MAN *is still snoring.*)

GANESHA (*singing*):

> "Good night, ladies,
> Good night, ladies,
> Good night, ladies,
> The milkman's on his way."

(*He pulls the drape across the stage. He looks at us. He puts his finger to his lips.*)

GANESHA: Good night.

(*He disappears through the curtain. The* MAN *is still snoring.*)